The
Feather Gang

Jon Hovis

INFINITY
PUBLISHING.COM

Copyright © 2009 by Jon Hovis

ISBN 0-7414-5188-3

Published by:

INFINITY
PUBLISHING.COM

1094 New DeHaven Street, Suite 100
West Conshohocken, PA 19428-2713
Info@buybooksontheweb.com
www.buybooksontheweb.com
Toll-free (877) BUY BOOK
Local Phone (610) 941-9999
Fax (610) 941-9959

Printed in the United States of America

Printed on Recycled Paper

Published February 2009

For His Glory.

I wish to thank my editor whose help was incalculable and Guy Zani Jr. for his valuable information regarding antique safes.

---Jon Hovis

Prologue

New York City, 1874.

The sniper sat on the roof of the four story building across from the bank. He was watching the lamplighter work his way down the street lighting all the gas streetlights. Soon it would be time to go and he could relax. The waiting always made his stomach cramp. Peering down along his Spencer rifle he noticed a police officer working his way along the other side of the street. The policeman was casually strolling along swinging his billyclub and looking in all the storefronts as he passed by. "I sure hope I don't have to shoot him," the sniper thought. That bank just happened to be occupied by his brother and cousin, who were helping themselves to whatever was in the safe.

The last time he had to shoot an officer of the law, their whole lives had changed. "Well, sort of," he thought. Back in his beloved Ireland, they had led a life of thievery as well. Making a living as a watchmaker, like their father, had proved to be too difficult for him and his brother; taking money from strangers seemed a much easier prospect. One day a copper had walked into the back room of the pub they were robbing on the outskirts of Limerick. As soon as he saw the cop, he reacted almost instantaneously and pulled the pistol that was in his belt. Cocking the hammer back and aiming at the same time, he then pulled the trigger.

Looking back, it was kind of humorous to watch the reactions of everyone. His brother was picking the lock on the desk drawer, and being totally engrossed in what he was doing, didn't hear the door open. He almost jumped out of his skin with the report of the shot. After seeing what had happened they were both trying to get out of the door, across the dead man, and away as fast as possible. Just before they got out through the door, the entire patronage from the pub rushed through from the front to see what had happened. He turned to look as everyone piled through and they all stopped for a second to take in the situation. Then all hell broke loose as the crowd shouted at them to stop and they took off running. Several men tried running after them, but had gotten out of the door too late to see which alleyway they had disappeared into. "Good thing we always have a getaway planned," he thought. Almost twenty men were scouring the streets looking for them, but they had already run several miles away and were hiding at their cousin's house near the river Shannon.

The next day their cousin came in from town and reported that the entire British authority was looking for them, both policemen and soldiers. Why that cop had walked in the back door of the pub they would never know, but his brother supposed that someone must have seen them go in and reported it. Next they had to decide what to do. Their cousin told them that they wouldn't be safe anywhere in the country after killing a policeman. After talking it over for a while, they decided to head for America. It wasn't too far to the sea, and if they left right away maybe they could get on a ship before the manhunt caught up to them.

Later that night they sneaked over through the shadows to their house and packed whatever they could fit into a gunnysack, then they made their way down to the river where their cousin was waiting in a small rowboat. He had said, "Can't make a good living here, so I'm going with you. I've heard there are great opportunities in the States for everyone. Besides, if they find out I helped you they'll also hang me." So they took turns rowing downriver all night and through the next day until they came to Kilrush.

There were not any passenger ships heading west for another two weeks, but they were able to book passage on a cargo ship that was leaving the next morning. They simply had to work on board to earn their keep. As soon as they were on board and underway, they breathed a sigh of relief; a new life in America and all the worries, hard living, and the law were behind them. His only regret was not being able to tell his father where they were going.

Of course his father was disappointed in them anyway. "Thank God your dear mother has been dead these many years," he would say. "She would die from the embarrassment of having two sons thievin' like you do."

His brother would retort "Da, you're the one who taught me how to open safes and pick locks, what did you think I would do with those skills?" Then an argument would start which his father would quickly end with "I could have the constable over here in two ticks." But still he missed his father.

A few weeks later found them in Boston among a few thousand other immigrants. Everyone was looking for work and a place to stay, and there was little from which to choose. It only took two months of disappointment and hardship to convince them that stealing was much easier than earning. They would hit a bank in Boston and then run to another city as fast as possible. The law never seemed to follow them past the county line. They made their way down the coast as far as Baltimore, stopping in at any bank on the way to make a withdrawal.

His brother was becoming so skilled at opening safes that some banks didn't even know they had been hit until days later. They always broke in at night, taking their time to avoid making any noise. He would sit outside somewhere and keep a lookout for trouble; usually across the street with his rifle at the ready. When his brother got the safe open, they would often times only take half of the cash. That way it looked normal for the bank employees the next morning. The only evidence that the safe had been opened was that his brother started leaving a feather from his hat in the safe. "Sort of his own little joke to play with their minds, or taunt them with his skill," he surmised.

After Baltimore, they took a train up to New York City. They had plenty of cash and they wanted to spend it and enjoy it. Unfortunately, after a year of living it up, the money was running out and here they were, at it again. The policeman he was watching had made his way to the front of the bank. At first he kept walking and the sniper let out a sigh of relief. But then the policeman turned and walked up the three steps to the front door. Peering inside for a few seconds, the policeman, with much excitation, turned and grabbed his whistle. Just as he was about to blow it, the sniper cursed under his breath and squeezed his finger on the trigger.

Chapter One

Colorado, 1877.

The man riding towards South Plains had his hat pulled down low, and his slicker wrapped tightly around his body. The driving rain had just stopped but the dark, looming clouds behind him threatened to drench him again. His horse, a Tennessee Pacer which he had picked up back east some years earlier, was trotting along at a pleasant gait not seeming to care at all about the weather. Both rider and horse looked the same. The man was tall and lean with a muscular build, dark brown hair and eyes and dressed all in black. The only contrast was a silver medallion on the side of his hat which matched the emblem on his holster. The horse was also dark brown with just a touch of a silver blaze on its forehead.

The train south from Denver had let him off a few miles back, at a small siding that was used mostly for loading cattle once a year at roundup. Eventually there was a line planned to head to town, but for now one had to walk or ride to get over to the train. As he drew closer to town, he could see that the community was growing. Anticipation for the coming railroad was helping the little one street collection of buildings. He could see several new houses going up, and even the train station was already being built. Getting closer he rode past several acres of corrals. The stockyard was the main reason this town existed. Every year the area cattle and sheep ranchers drove their livestock into town for auction, and then transport to the railroad which would take them from there to cities both east and west.

Just as he got to the edge of town, a huge bolt of lighting struck behind him. A half-second later the crack of thunder rippled through the town. Many of the townspeople looked towards the sound and they saw a stranger riding into town, dressed all in black, looking evil, and with a slight grin on his face. Steam was rising off his back and off the horse adding to the sinister look. "That's okay," he thought, "That's exactly the image I want to portray."

He rode slowly down the muddy street, looking at each building as he rode past, studying the layout of the town. As he rode by, the people who were out on the street stopped to watch him pass. They wondered who he was and what his business here was. From the low slung, tied down revolver and the two rifles slung along the saddle, it was obvious that he was not one of the cattle buyers who were arriving for the upcoming auction. Could he be a lawman? Or was he, as most feared, a gunman? If so, many were afraid of the trouble that could ensue.

When he reached the hotel, he got off his horse and tied it up to the hitching post in front of the yellow, two story building. Going inside he inquired about a room. The hotel owner, Samuel Blake, looked up from behind the counter. A man of slight build and receding hairline, he was somewhat overwhelmed by the imposing man who had just entered his establishment. "H'how may I help you?" he stammered. "Uh, mister…?"

"Black," the man answered. "Jake Black, and I want a room."

"Yes sir, yes sir," he nervously answered. "You are in luck, sir. I have just one room left. You see the auction is coming up and..."

"I don't care about your damn auction!" Black interrupted. "Just give me my key."

"Yes sir, right away sir." Blake answered. He grabbed the key off the pegboard behind him and handed it to Black. His hand was shaking so badly that the key was jingling. "If you will just sign the register and I'll need, um, one dollar for each night."

Black handed the man a five dollar note. "I'll be staying for a while," he said. Then he made his mark, an 'x' with a line through it, for a signature. He knew how to write, very well in fact, but he didn't want anyone to know that yet.

After putting his bedroll and gear in his room, Jake headed outside. "Time for this town to get to know me," he thought. Striding across the street he made his way to the Muddy Horse Saloon, his feet pounded across the boards on the porch as he came to the entrance. Pausing just one second to peer across the batwing doors, he pushed them open and walked in. "Well, this is disappointing," he said to no one in particular, "Where is everyone?" As he looked around the room, there were only two men in the room and one of them was asleep.

The bartender, known only as Tiny, looked over at him and said "Well, as it's only two in the afternoon, most people are workin'." Black took three long strides over to the bar, pulled out his Colt

Peacemaker, and put the barrel right under Tiny's nose.

"Are you trying to be smart with me?" he sneered.

"No sir," Tiny answered, "I was just answering your question. Would you care for a drink?"

"My name is Jake Black!" he shouted, waking up the sleeping man. As he put away his gun, he continued. "I'm the meanest S.O.B. this side of the Mississippi and I'll shoot any man who makes me mad or gets in my way. Now give me a whisky." The bartender gave him a drink and he gulped it down in one swallow. After tossing a nickel on the bar, he walked outside to have a look around.

Jake figured since most people were going about their business for now, he would do the same. He walked back over to the hotel where he had left his horse and got on. "Time to get a lay of the land," he said to himself.

Heading west out of town, he rode past a small church building on a rise just beyond the town, then towards the foothills that were a few miles away. There were several small ranches and farms along the road, but nothing much to get his attention. Most of the bigger ranches were much farther away.

After reaching a small stream and letting his horse take a drink, he turned around to ride back. He circled around to the south to see what was in that direction. Mostly it was just open prairie; a lot of grass and some areas with sage and cactus growing. Occasionally he would startle a jackrabbit and watch it run off in a zigzag pattern. As he got closer to town he came up behind the livery stables. "Might as well get a stall for Pacer."

When he rode up to the barn, a thin, scrawny young man walked out. Looking at the man Black said "Give my horse a good rub down, some oats, and your best stall. And make sure he has plenty of hay."

"Yes sir," the man replied. "My name is Colin Machen," he said as he stuck out his hand, "are ya new in town?"

"I don't care what your name is," Black replied, "just take good care of my horse." He then shoved three dollars into Colin's outstretched hand and walked off, leaving the stable hand looking after him with curiosity.

Black strolled over to the 'Plains Mercantile' which was a large building next to the hotel. The weathered sign out front indicated that the store had "everything you need". There was an old straight backed chair on the porch, in which he sat down, and then leaned back against the wall. Looking across the street he studied the various buildings and houses. Directly across from the mercantile was a clothing shop. It advertised a men's tailor and women's dressmaker, along with shoes and boots for all ages. Similar to most businesses, the living quarters were on the second floor. Next door to the dress shop was a watchmaker and gunsmith. "I'll need to go in there," he thought, "my gun needs to be looked at."

The next building down was the bank. "I'll have to really study that," he mused. It was a tall one story building, but almost as tall as the watchmaker's two story shop. Made of brick, it looked like a fortress.

The few windows had bars across them and the front door looked sturdy enough to stop a speeding locomotive. "Might as well go take a look inside," he decided. Black stood up and stepped down off the porch right in front of two men who were walking down the street. He didn't even look at them as he walked away but they stood there staring at him. "I wonder what his problem is?" one man said to the other.

"New in town from what I heard," the other replied, "Troublemaker from what some have been saying." They curiously watched Black as he strode over to the bank.

Opening the front door of the bank, Jake walked inside. His first impression of the interior was the same as his opinion of the outside. "A fortress," he mumbled to himself. The floors were made of stone, the walls were made of brick, and everything was twice as thick as normal. The bank tellers stood behind a tall counter with bars separating them from the customers. He couldn't even see through to the back where the safe should be. And then the biggest surprise was the armed guard standing in the corner. The man had two old '58 Army revolvers hanging from his gun belt, and he was holding a brand new, Winchester '73 repeating rifle. "Just like the one I have," he thought.

Jake looked at the guard who was looking at him and decided it was time to go. He turned around and walked out. Looking around he saw that there were now more men at the saloon, so he walked over and looked down at a man who was sitting on a rocking chair on the front porch. "I believe that's my chair," he growled at the man. At the same time he put his hand on his gun and flipped off the thong that held it down.

"Alright mister, you can have it," the man said. So Black dropped his tall frame down into the chair and grinned to himself.

A small crowd had gathered around the saloon watching this stranger with the bad attitude. Some were whispering among themselves, speculating as to what this man was up to. All of them, however, were giving him plenty of room to himself, staying well away. Off to one side, several boys were trying to goad each other into saying something to Black. One boy, about twelve years old, said he would do it if the others paid him a nickel each. They agreed so he walked up to Black and said, "Hey mister, are you really the meanest man this side of the Mississippi?" Black looked at the kid and gestured to him to come closer.

"Come here," he said. The kid stepped forward. Black then lifted up his leg and kicked the kid square in the chest so that he fell backwards, off the porch, and into the muddy street. "Does that answer your question?" he asked. He then chuckled to himself as the crowd stood there in shock.

One man shouted, "Hey, you can't do that!"

"Who's going to stop me?" Black shouted back, laughing again. Then a large, muscular man stepped around the crowd.

"Maybe I will. Let's see if you can pick on someone a little bigger." The crowd started getting excited at the prospects of a fight.

"Someone had better get the sheriff," one man said.

More people started gathering around as word of a fight spread. The mean stranger named Black against Joey Mengel. Joey was the strongest man in town because he was the blacksmith. Swinging a hammer all day and forging metal had built the man into an ox. As he moved forward he took off his shirt. He was a hairy man but you could still see the muscles rippling underneath that furry mat. Black stood up and sized up the man before him. He was built like the anvil he used all day, but was probably slow.

Black had faced many men before and he knew what he could do in a fight. He had boxed some while in school and he knew how to take a punch. Even strong men would go down with one punch if they had never been hit before. And Black could hit. His muscles were lean and strong and fast. Plus, his long reach would be an advantage. Since Black didn't know this man he really didn't want to fight him, but this would shore up his image as a troublemaker.

Black slipped off his gun belt and rolled up his sleeves. He stepped down to the street where the crowd had formed a circle. Many had already placed bets on the outcome, and most had bet on Joey.

The two men raised their fists and were slowly circling each other. Black waited until the late afternoon sun was behind him and temporarily blinding his opponent, and then launched out with a straight punch to the blacksmith's nose. Joey never even saw it coming and the punch hit him so hard that he almost blacked out. But he quickly shook it off and swung a punch of his own. Black easily stepped out of the way and at the same time crossed with his left. The punch hit Joey across the cheek but the man barely moved. "This might be harder than I thought," Black surmised. Joey was getting angrier as they danced around and he couldn't land any punches; swing after swing met with air as Black dodged each punch. Changing tactics Joey charged at Black like a bull, catching him by surprise. Both men fell to the ground with Joey straddling Black around his waist. The blacksmith smiled as he thought now he would pound some punches into his face. But Black was ready for him; his experience fighting Indians had prepared him with some wrestling moves. As Joey was about to smash a fist into his face like a hammer landing on an anvil, Black swung his leg up and around the front of his neck. Pushing his leg backwards, it took the blacksmith down with it. Black then rolled over and swung his arm down on the man's chest with a blow that would have broken some ribs on any other man.

Next Black stood up and was about to kick the man when a deafening shot rang out. Everyone froze in place including Jake Black, standing there with his leg back, ready to swing. Looking back over his shoulder, he saw a man standing several feet away, shotgun smoking from the shot he had fired into the air. "That's enough, you. I'm Sheriff Adam Murphy and you are under arrest."

Chapter Two

The sheriff was an older man with a pot belly and old ragged clothes. His shabby appearance was not due to incompetence or laziness, but years of wear and tear upholding the law. He marched his two prisoners down the street by gunpoint to the jail which was located at the end of town. He had already taken Jake Black's gun belt and then put handcuffs on both men. When they reached the sheriff's office, which was the front room of the jailhouse, he removed the handcuffs and then put each man in a separate cell.

Black walked into his cell and turned around with his arms leaning against the bars. "Sheriff," he said, "don't you think you should have this also?" He held out a small derringer which he kept inside a small holster inside his boot.

"Where did you get that?" Sheriff Murphy asked.

"It was in my boot," Black replied.

"Well what else do you have in there?"

"Nothing," he replied. "However, you may also want this." He reached into his other boot and pulled out a small, double edged dagger. He flicked it forward and it stuck into the worn, wooden desk.

Sheriff Murphy stared at him for a few seconds. "Anything else I should know about?"

"Nope, that's it." Black said. "I would like to talk to you privately though, when you have a minute." He reached into his pocket and pulled out his Marshal's badge and showed it so that the sheriff was the only one who could see it.

Murphy looked at the badge for a second then back at Black. "Give me a bit to take care of some business and then we'll talk."

Meanwhile, behind the barn, the members of the Feather Gang were meeting. They occasionally met together to plan their next move, but usually did not associate with each other around town.

"Anything to report?" the leader asked.

His brother who was working at the town post office replied, "Nothing in the mail. There are a lot of people in town for the auction though."

"Well that's good for us; lots of distractions so we can do what we came here to do. This one will make us rich, boys," he continued. "Most of the planning is done; all we have to do is wait."

His cousin said, "That new guy in town might be trouble, 'cept of course that he's in jail right now."

"Don't worry about him," the leader replied. "One man alone can't ruin our plans. The next thing we need to do is move the supplies into place. Do you have everything ready?" he asked, looking at his cousin.

"Yep," he replied, "I'll bring them over tomorrow night when the moon will be dark. That way no one will see anything."

"Sounds good," the leader said, "I'll be ready for you around ten 'o clock." With that they each walked away in a different direction, just in case someone was watching.

Two hours later the sheriff walked back into his office. He went over to the cell where Joey was already asleep. Opening the cell, he went in and shook the man awake. "Okay, Joe, you can go. I talked to all the witnesses, and they explained that you were just sticking up for the kid. You've done your time for disorderly conduct, and you can go."

"Well, thanks sheriff, but what about him?" he asked, pointing at Black.

"He'll have to spend a couple of nights here for instigating all this trouble. You get along now; your wife will have supper for you."

Murphy looked at the man in the other cell for a while, trying to size him up. Black just stared back. The sheriff grabbed a plate of food which he had put on his desk and handed it through the bars. "Alright, you wanted to talk; let's talk. You might start by explaining that badge you showed me earlier."

Black was hungrily spooning down the grub and took a minute before replying. "Sheriff, my name isn't Black. It's Silver. United States Deputy Marshal Jake Silver." He took a minute to let that sink in while he finished his food.

The sheriff looked at him and asked, "Then why in blazes are you runnin' around my town acting like a darn fool?"

Marshal Jake Silver leaned back on his cot and said, "Sheriff, I'm working undercover. I am on the trail of a gang of outlaws that have been robbing banks from here all the way to Boston. If you have a minute I'll tell you all about it." Murphy, still a little suspicious, shrugged his shoulders and gestured for him to continue.

"A few years ago," Jake began, "A policeman was killed in New York City while a bank was being robbed. The bandits got away, but they left something that gave investigators something to go on; a feather. After looking further into the case, it was determined that this gang had hit a dozen banks all along the east coast. In every instance, the robbery occurred at night, the locks on the bank doors were expertly picked, the safe was opened as opposed to blasted, and the thieves left a nice little hat feather inside the safe. No one," he continued, "has ever seen these guys. They operate in a stealthy method so as to avoid attracting attention to themselves, and we don't even know how many members are in this gang.

"Well, ever since the shooting, they have started making their way west. The only difference in their methods is that instead of hitting big banks in large cities, they are targeting small cities with small banks. I have a theory that once they rob a bank, they head across state lines to a larger city and lay low for a while."

"What makes you think they are here in South Plains?" the sheriff asked.

Jake paused to take a sip from his coffee before replying. "Well, we think they were in Dodge City before hitting a bank in Lamar. If you draw a line directly west from there then they should be here next. I admit it's just a guess, but there are several reasons which brought me to that conclusion. First, there is a bank here, and it has never been successfully robbed before. Second, the upcoming cattle auction means that that bank will be full of money. And lastly, they can't go any further west without hitting the Rocky Mountains which means that after this job, I figure that they will probably want to head to a larger city, most likely Denver."

"Okay," the sheriff said, "If that is all true, it still doesn't explain your strange behavior since you rode into town."

"Well, like I said earlier, I'm working undercover. If this gang knows that I'm in town, they may forget their plans and take off. I figure this way I can go around town without raising any alarms. My plan from the start was to let them hit this bank and we'll catch them in the act. I believe that this is the only way we will catch them."

"Well Marshal," Sheriff Murphy replied, "I didn't live this long by believing every tall tale that comes my way. How do I know that you are telling me the truth?"

Silver answered, "Send a telegram in the morning to the district marshal's office in Denver. Ask them the name of who they sent to your town and the answer will be my name. Do you think that will satisfy your skepticism?"

"Yes, I believe it will. And just to be on the safe side, I'll be keeping you behind those bars until that telegram comes back."

"That's fine sheriff," Silver said, "It would look wrong if you let me out early anyway." Handing back his dinner plate, Jake turned to lie down for the night.

He started thinking about his trip down from Denver and how he ended up here.

Three days earlier, his boss, Marshal J.T. Allen had called him into his office to discuss this case. "Silver," he began, "you are my best deputy."

"Sounds like you're setting me up for something," Jake interrupted.

"It's a big case," Allen continued, "A gang of bank bandits that no one can seem to catch." He then proceeded to explain all the details of the case.

"Sounds intriguing," Silver said, "Why me?"

"I need someone who is clever enough to outthink these guys," J.T. replied, "You have a good mind for figuring out things."

Silver had then poured over all the known facts of the case as well as reading newspaper articles about the robberies. He noticed the trends and similarities between all the separate occurrences and made his plans. The next day he bought a train ticket as well as arranging for space on the train for his horse.

He was glad for the opportunity to take on this challenge because he prided himself with the ability to use his mind as well as the other tools of his trade, such as his muscles and his guns.

Having been raised in Pennsylvania in a well-to-do family, he had been able to attend all the best schools. From an early age, he had roamed the woods near his home hunting squirrels with his flintlock musket; his father would take him deer hunting on occasion. Attending a private boarding school gave him wonderful opportunities to learn a variety of subjects. He enjoyed music, history, and reading adventure books, but would have preferred to be outside instead of studying Latin and literature. When he was older and entered the university, he excelled in the boxing league and other sports. His parents had wanted him to study business law to follow in his father's footsteps but he was still undecided.

One big event came about that helped make up his mind…the War Between the States. After one year of civil war, he decided to leave school and sign up. He was able to use his skills to be a sniper and a spy; skills that kept him off the front lines. Standing in a field in a line with a hundred men facing a hundred other men all shooting back at you didn't seem like a good idea to him. For a young lad, it all seemed like fun and adventure until the killing started, but by then it was too late, he was already in. Working behind the scenes offered him the thrills and adventure that he craved. When the war ended, it seemed a natural progression to sign up as a deputy marshal and work as a lawman in the untamed west.

The next morning, the sheriff walked into the jail studying a piece of paper that he held in his hand. He walked over to the cell where Silver was lying on his cot and studied him for a moment. When Jake opened his eyes, Sheriff Murphy said, "Your story checks out, you are free to go."

Silver sat up yawning, and then started pulling on his boots. "I'm going to need your help, if you'd be willing."

"I'll do whatever I can to assist you," Murphy said, "but I'm still not convinced that anyone can get that bank."

Jake replied, "That's okay, I can use someone to bounce ideas off of and who will argue the counterpoint with me."

Sheriff Murphy opened the cell door and let Marshal Silver out. They walked over to his desk and sat down. "Tell me about the bank," Silver requested, "I know what's inside the front door, but I need to know what is behind the wall that is behind the tellers."

"Well, I haven't even seen it myself, but Paul Schmidt, the owner of the bank, described it to me one day. The walls are double thick brick, and the safe is encased in brick on three sides. That reminds me, when they brought that safe in here, it took twenty men just to offload it."

Silver asked, "What about entry into the building? I only saw one door and that was at the front."

"That's right," Murphy answered, "They built that building around the safe and the only way in or out is the front door. As far as I know, there are a couple of desks and an office for Schmidt and that big safe back there."

Silver sat back in his chair and thought for a moment. "One more thing I'll need from you; get me a list of every person here in South Plains who is new in town over the past eighteen months."

Murphy looked at him amazed, "Why that's half the population! But I suppose if that's what you want.

It'll take me some time to get a list together but I'll work on it straightaway."

"Good," Silver replied, "I'll be back in a couple of hours so that we can go over your list. Meanwhile, I'm going to head over to the bank and study it for a while to see if I can come up with any ideas."

Chapter Three

The sun was high in the bright, blue sky, without any clouds to block the rays from beating down. Thirty feet away stood a man, dirty, sweating in the heat. His hat was pulled down low which hid his eyes. His face, covered in a scraggly beard, was weathered and wrinkled. The man was chewing on a stub from a cigar that had gone out at least an hour ago. His clothes were threadbare and had sweat stains around his armpits. His right hand was still, hovering just over his revolver. The thong had been slipped off, and just a split second would be required to pull the gun out of the holster.

Silver stood looking at the man. His own gun, a Colt Peacemaker was brand new. The holster was still new as well, and the leather was stiff and rough. "Would the gun come out smoothly?" he wondered. As he stared down the stranger, a trickle of sweat ran down the side of his face. He dared not wipe it away as the other man might draw at any time. A fly started buzzing around his face, distracting him. Annoyed, he raised his hand to swat it away. Just then the other man went for his gun. In a split second, the stranger's gun had cleared his holster and he raised it up to fire. He drew back the hammer and at the same time pulled the trigger. Silver stood there watching everything happen; stunned into inaction, he couldn't will himself to pull his own gun. He watched the bullet coming towards him… "That's strange," he thought, "How come I can see the bullet?" Just before it hit him, someone shouted from beside him. He woke with a start and looked groggily around him. "Dreamin' again," he said, looking sheepishly around to see if anyone was paying him any mind. "I've got to stop doing that," he thought.

Marshal Silver had been sitting across the street from the bank, studying the layout, going over in his mind different possibilities that the criminal mind might consider for getting inside. Based on what he knew from the newspaper articles, the Feather Gang always picked the locks on the doors, and used some sort of extraordinary skills in opening the safe. The only way he could imagine getting this safe open was to blast it with dynamite. The sheriff had told him that the safe was supposed to be the best in the world and was impossible to open by any safecracker. "It will be interesting to see how they do it," he thought. He figured his only advantage would be to whittle down the list of names the sheriff was working on to just a few suspects. That way he could keep an eye on them and wait for them to make their move.

Jake walked slowly over to the sheriff's office. He didn't want it to look like he had business there. Upon entering the building, he saw Sheriff Murphy working at his desk, writing down names on a piece of paper. Murphy looked up as he walked in. "Almost done Marshal," he said, handing him another piece of paper, "I have your list ready for you, but I'm working on another list for you. This one is a list of all the men who have come into town in just the past week for the auction. I figured you would want these names separate."

Silver took the list from him and sat down to study it. He read all the names, of which there were about thirty. Then he went back over the list more carefully and started to note which ones he wanted to check out more thoroughly. He discounted any married folks, and anyone with children first. Also, there were many who worked on ranches outside of town. He figured anyone casing the bank would need to work in town, and have a reason to be around full time. Besides, most of the ranch hands were so busy with the roundups, they wouldn't have time to get away, plus they would be missed if they spent too much time in town and off the range. Jake looked back over his revised list and discussed it with the sheriff.

"I've got seven names here that I'd like to investigate. First is the tailor, Paul Morton."

"Actually, he is married," said the sheriff, "His wife is the dressmaker, but she didn't take his name for some reason. I think it's because she is his cousin or something."

"Okay, scratch that one for now. Next on the list is the freight wagon driver, Dennis Jackson. What do you know about him?" Silver asked.

"Not much," Murphy replied, "But he is a good worker from what I've seen. He doesn't seem to socialize much."

Silver considered that, "Good, we'll keep an eye on him. Next, the blacksmith, whom I've already met,

Joe Mengel. Didn't you say something about him having a wife?"

"Oh yeah," the sheriff replied, "He is married; I forgot to indicate that. His wife has lived here most of her life so I didn't add her to the list. They got hitched here just a month ago."

"Fine, we'll cross his name off also," Silver said. "The next name is Colin Machen, stable hand."

"Yeah, another one who keeps to himself. Friendly when you talk to him though,"

"We'll also keep him on the list," Jake said. "Next is the post office worker, Daniel O'Connell, and the watchmaker and gunsmith William O'Connell. Same surname; are they related?"

The sheriff thought about it, "No, at least not that anyone has ever said. They did show up about the same time though."

"That's interesting," Silver said, "Two brothers could definitely be part of the same gang."

"The last name here then is Samuel Blake, the hotel owner. How well do you know him?"

"Fairly well actually," the sheriff began, "He likes to sit in the saloon and preach to us sinners; drives people crazy. I have to go in after a while and tell him to leave. He also covers the preachin' duties for most of the month at the church out there on the hill." Murphy pointed out to the far side of town and continued, "The circuit preacher only comes by about once a month so he fills in the rest of the time. Most of the folks seem to like him; has a great singing voice as well. I heard him sing myself just last Sunday."

Silver asked, "You go to church, Sheriff?"

"Yep," he replied simply, "on occasion."

"Well," Silver said, "I suppose our Christian brother most likely is not a bank robber, but it would make for a good cover. I'll keep an eye on him just the same, for now."

Silver got up to leave; Murphy looked up and asked, "Is there anything else you need me to do?"

"No, not for now, just keep my cover a secret. As the auction draws nearer, I may need your help to stakeout the bank. Hopefully I'll have the list of suspects down to three or four by then. For now I'm going to head out and see the one O'Connell fellow."

Deputy Marshal Silver made his way back down the street to the shop of the watchmaker and gunsmith. Several people eyed him warily as he walked down the street. He ignored them for now, satisfied that no one knew who he really was.

He stepped up to the front walk and into the shop. There were pocket watches and clocks of every sort on display along one wall. The other side of the shop had several rifles and a variety of hand guns for sale. Silver was looking over the selection when William O'Connell came in from the workshop.

"Nice selection," Silver said to the man, "It must have taken you quite some time to put this together."

William considered this man in his shop for a few seconds before replying. "Not really, I bought this shop last year from a man who was heading to California. He left me most of his inventory. Is there something I can help you with?"

Silver replied, "Yeah, I have this derringer," which he pulled out of his boot, "The barrel is difficult to move, and only one barrel will fire." He handed the gun to O'Connell.

The gunsmith looked over the gun. "Nice gun; a silver plated Remington, .41 caliber with an over under barrel. It looks like it just needs a good cleaning. Seeing as you keep it in your boot, it probably gets a lot of dust and dirt inside. There is a cam on the hammer which alternates fire between the barrels, and it is most likely clogged with dirt. I'll disassemble it and clean it; should only take an hour or so."

Silver left the shop and walked back over to the hotel. "Better make sure I still have a room," he thought. He stopped halfway across the street after hearing a commotion. Looking down to the end of town, a large herd of cattle had just arrived. The cowboys herded the cows into the corrals, whooping and hollering. The auction was only a few days away now, so every day was going to get busier.

Silver walked into the hotel to find the owner behind the desk. "You had better still have my room," he growled at the man. Samuel Blake's eyes went wide at seeing the man he thought of as Black.

"Oh, yes sir," he replied, "You paid for a room and it is still yours. Do you plan on staying in it tonight?" he asked, and then immediately regretted the words.

Silver glared at the man and leaned over the desk. "What did you say?"

"I, I, I hope you enjoy your stay," he stammered.

"That's what I thought you said," Silver replied. Standing back up straight he said, "I understand you like to preach to sinners; maybe I'll come to church on Sunday and hear what you have to say. What do you think about that?"

"Well," Blake answered, "All are welcome in the house of God." His hand was shaking as he handed Silver the room key. The marshal figured that this man most likely was not the criminal type.

"Can't keep his composure under fire," he surmised as he left the office. He went to his room to rest for a while and then figured he would head back over to pick up his gun.

As Jake Silver lay on his bed, he thought about the gunsmith/watchmaker. The man was not at all intimidated by his presence, plus his manner was cool and composed during the entire visit. He could tell that O'Connell had been checking him out just as much as the reverse. Also, with the shop right next to the bank, his location alone was suspect. If the other O'Connell in town has similar looks and mannerisms, then he figured that he had found at least two members of the gang.

After a short nap, Silver got up to go and retrieve his gun. As he walked into the shop, the gunsmith was waiting for him. "Ah, Mister Black, I have your derringer all ready for you. There was a bit of lint in the hammer mechanism, and the barrel hinge was really dirty. I stripped it down and cleaned it and now it works just fine."

He handed the gun over and Silver looked it over. "Looks like you polished the outside as well?" he asked. The gun shone like it was brand new again.

"Yes sir," O'Connell said, "And that will be fifty cents."

"Fifty cents!" the marshal exploded, "For an hours worth of work?"

O'Connell didn't even flinch. "Yes sir, fifty cents." He stood his ground and held out his hand for the money.

"Well, I guess since you also polished the silver it's worth it." Jake grumbled. He slapped the coins down in the man's outstretched hand and walked out. His suspicions had been confirmed...this man was definitely the one for whom he was looking.

Chapter Four

It was getting late in South Plains and the shadows were long across the street. Deputy Marshal Jake Silver headed over to the restaurant to get some supper. His stomach had been growling at him for some time now and a big meal would really hit the spot. The lights were on in the dining hall and the building was full of people. With the extra visitors in town and the cowboys just in from the cattle drive, the place was packed.

Jake stood in the open doorway looking around at the crowd. The mood was jovial as conversations and good food were consumed. The wait staff was running back and forth between the kitchen and tables, trying to keep food on the tables for the hungry crowd.

As people started to notice him standing there, a hush started to spread across the room. Soon, every eye was on him, wondering what he was going to do. Not a single table was available, and most every seat was taken. Silver had a slight grin on his face after seeing how everyone reacted to his presence. He wondered if anyone would dare make a move.

Just in front of him, there was a small table with only one occupant. Staring back at him was the most beautiful woman he had ever seen. She had long blonde hair tucked up under a bonnet, a pert little nose that was slightly upturned at the end, and the most striking blue eyes he had ever seen. The only empty chair in the place was at her table. The woman stood up. She was medium tall with a slim figure, wearing a plain blue dress that fit her so well that it made Jake almost forget who he was.

The woman gestured to the chair opposite her and said, "Sir, would ye care to sit down?" Jake realized that he had been staring at her with his mouth open along with the rest of the crowd.

Regaining his composure he said, "Yes ma'am." Putting his grin back in place, he sat down. Taking off his hat, he placed it to the side and introduced himself. "Jake Black, ma'am, and you are?"

"Rachel Kilbourne, and it's miss, ye can drop the ma'am business."

"Yes ma'am," Jake replied, "So how is it that you aren't scared of me like the rest of the town here?"

Rachel looked around the room as the patrons slowly started returning to their meals, "Mr. Black, I believe it is my Christian duty as a Quaker to be hospitable to all men, even such as yourself. It would not be right to make thee stand there and wait when there is a perfectly good chair here in which to sit."

"Well Miss Kilbourne, I and my growling stomach appreciate your hospitality." Silver studied his dinner companion for a minute while he waited for his meal. "Quaker huh? I didn't realize there were any 'Friends' out here. What made you come out west?"

"My mother, on her deathbed, after being quiet for three days and nights, had a vision. In her vision, she told us that we should leave after she died, and head west. Two days later that is exactly what we did. My father and two brothers packed up all our belongings, and by God's providence we ended up here."

"Do you live here in town," he asked.

"No," she replied, "We have a small farm a mile outside of town. We also raise chickens, many of which we sell to the restaurant here."

Just then their food arrived, so they fell into silence while they ate. When he had finished, Jake, with a little curiosity and some desire to taunt her asked, "So how did you know that this is where you were to settle, and now that you are here, what does the good Lord want you to do?"

"Mister Black," Rachel began, "One does not question the direction of the Lord. This is where our wagon broke a wheel hub, so this is where we stayed. As to His work," she continued, "Perhaps He sent us here to save thy soul which appears to be as black as your name!" Silver couldn't help himself and laughed out loud. She would be in for a shock when she found out who he really was.

Finished with his meal, Jake got up to leave. "Friend Rachel," he said, "Perhaps you would like to have dinner with me tomorrow evening as well so you can continue the Lord's work?"

She looked up at him disdainfully, "I think not, Mr. Black; ye are only interested in food, not God."

Jake laughed again and said, "No, Miss Kilbourne, I'm interested in you." And with that he grabbed his hat and walked out, leaving her staring at his back with her mouth open.

Later that evening, as most of the townsfolk were settling down for the night, or having that last drink at the saloon, the Feather Gang met behind the shop. The leader opened the back door to the workshop and gestured for the other two men to bring over the supplies.

They carried over four long boards on their shoulders and set them up against the building. Going back behind the stables they retrieved a block and tackle, some short poles, and several lengths of rope. They carried the poles and tackle upstairs to the living quarters. In the front room, there was a trap door that had been cut into the ceiling which led out onto the roof. It was a pitched roof so they had to be careful not to fall off, and fortunately there was a false front on the building so they were hidden from anyone who may have looked up from the street. They left the supplies in the room, but took the rope up with them. It was lowered down to the ground where the leader was waiting. After he tied the rope around the long boards he gave a soft whistle. The other two hoisted the boards up to the roof and laid them out along the edge. A few well placed nails, that had been driven in earlier, would hold the boards in place until they were ready to use.

They met back down in the shop and reviewed the plan. "Any problems or issues?" the leader asked.

"No," they both replied.

"Good. What about that Black fellow?"

"He has just been wondering around town from what I've seen," the cousin replied. "I did see him come in here today, what did he want?"

"Just getting a gun cleaned," William replied. "I'm suspicious of him though; he was asking too many questions. We had better keep an eye on him, although I don't think he will affect our plans in any way.

"Everything is in place, so we'll lay low tomorrow," the leader continued, "We'll meet here on Thursday evening and carry out our plan; any questions?" The other two men shook their heads, and then they left by the back door and made their way home.

William reviewed the plan again in his head. He was meticulous in his planning and had every detail worked out. This job was to be different than all the rest. They had come a long way since the old country. Using the same formula for so long had been successful up until now, but he was sure that eventually they would get caught if they continued. This plan was different. He wanted to live out his life in comfort and luxury, and so far none of the bank jobs had provided enough. This time all that was going to change; no more running from the law and always looking over their shoulders. He had been planning this for a longer period of time than ever before; they had invested almost six months and plenty of money to buy the building next to the bank. The method was different and the score was going to be huge, and his life of ease was going to start in just a few more weeks. They had their sights set on San Francisco, it was populated enough for them to blend in, and far enough away from the rest of the country so they would never have the law looking for them there. He imagined himself going to lavish parties with the upper class, eating the best food, and living the easy life of the rich.

William O'Connell sat down at his desk and took out a piece of paper. He wrote out a telegram to send in the morning. It stated that a business was for sale, inventory included. "No more tinkering with these damned watches like my father," he said to himself. He put away his pen and turned in for the night, satisfied that everything was well and going according to plan.

Chapter Five

On Wednesday morning, Jake got up slowly, stretching to get himself going, and then dressed. He went down to the hotel office to turn in his key to the owner. Samuel Blake was intimidated as usual, but Jake ignored him and walked out, tossing the key on the desk as he passed.

Going over to the restaurant to get some coffee and eggs to start his day, Jake planned out his next move. The room was only half full this morning as most folks had already eaten and were about their business. He sat down at a table next to the front window so he could watch the world go by and ordered his food.

After the waitress left, he thought about the men left on the list the sheriff had given him. He would definitely check out the other O'Connell on the list; having the same surname as the watchmaker was a dead giveaway. The stable hand and the guy working at the freight depot would come next.

When he finished his eggs, he left some money on the table and walked over to the sheriff's office. Entering the building, he found Sheriff Murphy sitting at his desk. The sheriff looked up and greeted him, "How are you this morning, Marshal?"

"I'm fine, Sheriff," he replied. "I was wondering if I could borrow some paper and use your pen? I need to write a letter."

Murphy agreed and handed over the supplies. "What are you up to this morning?" he asked.

"I need an excuse to visit the post office, so I'm going to write a letter; Daniel O'Connell works there and he was on your list. I also wanted to ask you about the Kilbourne family; what do you know about them?"

"The Kilbournes?" The sheriff asked, "Good family, devoutly religious. They have a successful farm and are hard working. You aren't suspecting them of anything, are you?"

"No," Silver replied. "I met Rachel Kilbourne last night and was just wondering."

After writing a few short lines on the paper, he then folded it up and addressed it to his boss' home in Denver in order to keep his suspect from finding out anything. Then he walked out of the jail and over to the post office. Just behind the jail, a man watched from around the corner of the building.

Silver entered the post office. It was a small building with a counter, desk, and a wall filled with pigeon holes for holding the incoming mail. Daniel O'Connell was sitting at the desk when the marshal walked in. He turned to see who had entered and when he saw Silver his eyes narrowed with suspicion. Standing up Daniel asked, "What can I do for you?" His hand had gone behind his back when he stood up. The marshal had noticed this but remained calm. The man most likely had a gun tucked behind his belt, but Jake knew if he pulled it, he could outdraw him.

Silver held out the letter in his left hand and said, "I would like to mail this." His right hand was resting on the grip of his gun just in case he needed it.

Daniel relaxed and smiled. "Of course, sir," he said and took the letter. "Where is it heading?"

"Denver," Silver said flatly. The postman took a stamp and put it on the letter.

"Should get there in a few days; head out on the train tomorrow, that'll be three cents."

The marshal put down the coins and left the building. As he went out the door he turned and looked back at the postman. Daniel O'Connell was looking at the letter, studying the address, but then Daniel noticed out of the corner of his eye that Black had not left the doorway and he quickly put the letter down in the bag.

Silver went across the walkway and leaned against a post and considered his visit. The man was similar in appearance to William, and had the same faint Irish accent. He had no doubt at all that these two were brothers.

With that task done, Silver made his way down the street to the freight office. At the end of the street there was a cloud of dust heading his way so he stepped inside the mercantile. Another herd of cattle was being driven into the corrals at the end of town, stirring up the dirt and causing no small commotion. The man watching from the end of the street made a note of all this and headed behind the buildings to get back to work.

Silver watched the cattle drive through the window of the mercantile. The cows were mostly Texas Longhorns. They had different variations of colors and sizes and some even had horns that spanned six feet or more. The herd being driven in today looked to be several hundred head. They had been free roaming all year long, fattening up on the long grass of the eastern plains. With the coming of the railroad, long cattle drives were going to come to an end soon. Many of the local ranchers were crossbreeding with, or switching to Hereford and Angus stock, which were easier to raise and have more meat on their bones. The longhorns were better suited for the trail but had a more wild temperament.

Silver waited inside the store for things to settle down. The stock yards were right behind the freight depot and there were still a few steers running loose around the street. The cowboys were chasing them down and lassoing them one by one. Soon all was in order so he turned around to leave.

The owner of the mercantile was looking at him so he glared at the man and yelled, "What?" The owner looked down right away and so Jake went outside. "There are going to be a lot of people around here that I'll need to apologize to when this is all done," he thought.

The freight depot was a large building with loading docks along the back and one side of the building. The sheriff told him that it was operated by the Paine family, and that Dennis Jackson was employed by them. They ran freight wagons south to the smaller towns that were too far away from the rail line. The business was in a good position to handle all the supply that would come into town once the railroad spur was put in.

Walking into the office he found Silas Paine sitting at a desk, sorting through shipping papers. Silas looked up and saw, with some surprise, who was standing in his office. He had heard about this man called Black and could not imagine what he would want here. Silas Paine was an older man, lean and muscled from years of hard work. He had handled plenty of misfits and troublemakers in his day; men trying to rob his wagons along the trail, and shysters who wanted to avoid paying for services, so he was not too concerned about this man in his office. Looking back down, Silas continued thumbing through his paperwork.

After a minute had passed, he looked up again and asked, "Can I help you?"

Marshal Silver grinned. He had been sizing up this man and could tell that he wasn't someone to be messed with, so he asked plainly, "I'm looking for Dennis Jackson, is he here?"

Paine wasn't going to volunteer any information to this troublemaker so he simply replied, "No."

Silver asked, "Where can I find him?"

"Look mister," Silas replied, "I don't know who you are, and I don't know what you want with Dennis. So why don't you just…"

Before he could finish his sentence, Jake Silver had pulled his gun and was pointing it straight at Paine's nose. The gun had appeared so fast that he didn't even see it coming. His eyes went wide and he opened and closed his mouth several times without saying anything. "Now," Silver said, "Let's start again. Where is Jackson?"

Silas replied, "I don't want him to get into any trouble, he is the best worker I have."

Jake slowly pulled back on the hammer. The gun clicked as the cylinder rotated to the next chamber.

Paine said, "He is over at the train depot, several miles east…"

"I know where it is," Jake interrupted, "Don't worry; I just want to talk to him." Lowering the hammer back down, Jake spun the pistol around on his finger before dropping it back into its holster. He turned and walked out. "One more name to add to the apology list," he said to himself as he headed over to get his horse.

Walking into the stable, Silver found his horse. The stable hand was nowhere to be seen for some reason, so he got his saddle and bridle and saddled up his horse by himself. Next he stopped by the hotel and retrieved his rifles and then headed out of town. From the loft of the stable, Colin Machen watched the man ride off until he was over the rise and too distant to see.

Jake let his horse run most of the way to let it expend some extra energy, and then he held it to a fast trot for which the breed was well known. It was a smooth gait that the horse could hold for hours if necessary, but he was coming up to the train depot. As he came closer, Silver could see the storage shed where Dennis Jackson was working. The young man was loading up a wagon with supplies that had been stored there from the last freight train. The depot also had two platforms on each side of the tracks, one side was next to the stock yard for loading cattle, and there was a water tower for the locomotive.

Riding up to where Jackson was working, Silver swung off his horse. Dennis looked at the stranger and said "Hello".

"Are you Dennis Jackson?" Silver asked.

"Yes," he answered. Dennis took off his hat and wiped his brow. "How did you know?"

Silver replied, "Mr. Paine said you were out here. Will you be loading the cattle cars this Saturday?"

"Oh, you must be from one of the cattle companies," Dennis guessed. "No sir," he continued, "I'll be out delivering these supplies. I've got two towns to get to this week, plus bringing back freight that's headin' to Denver. I won't be back 'til Sunday."

The marshal talked with the man for several more minutes before heading back to town. This obviously was not one of the gang. He was going to be out of town during the auction, and there was no telltale Irish accent. Also, he didn't figure someone who didn't like to work for a living would have a job like Jackson held.

Riding slowly back to town, Jake considered his next move. There was only one name left on the list, Colin something, the stable hand. He was unsure of how many members were in this gang. It could be just two, but most outlaws he had dealt with in the past had more members. However, this gang liked to operate differently than most so anything was possible. Regardless, he decided he was going to need some help. He would need to keep an eye on his suspects the day, and night, of the auction, and since there was more than one suspect, he needed an extra set of eyes. After considering it for a while, he knew the perfect men to ask.

As evening approached, Jake rode west out of town. He still had a couple of hours of sunlight left, which he figured would be enough. He rode past the small church on the rise, and then a cabin which was abandoned. After a mile or so, he came to a gate leading up to a farmhouse. Passing through the gate, Jake rode up to the house. There was a barn off to the side and a dozen chicken houses. The fields behind the house had corn and wheat which was golden brown and just about ready to harvest.

As he drew up his horse at the hitching post, Rachel Kilbourne walked out to see who had ridden up. When she saw who it was she put her hands on her hips, looked straight into his eyes and said, "Mister Black, I told thee quite plainly that I was not going to have supper with thee this evening."

Silver laughed and replied, "Friend Rachel, whatever gave you the idea that I was here to see you?"

She looked back at him with a confused look on her face, "Then who, may I ask, are ye here to see?"

Jake grinned back at her and said, "I am here to see your brothers; are they around somewhere?"

Still confused, Rachel answered, "Yes, they are working in the barn."

"Why thank you," Jake said. He tipped his hat to her and turned his horse to ride over to the barn.

Rachel stood there fuming at the audacity of this man. "How could he be so rude?" And then she was mad at herself for caring about him in any way at all. Sure, he was handsome and confident, but the way he acted was so un-Christian like. All at once she decided to forget this man, so she turned and went back into the house to continue with the dinner preparations.

Silver pulled up his horse at the barn. The building was beautifully built with timber framing and hand sawn boards. The carpentry work was expertly done and he could see that it was built with care and pride. Inside the barn everything was clean and in its place. Looking around for a minute but not seeing anyone, Jake walked around behind the barn where he had heard some noise.

There were three men; all had sweat stains from working hard. They were digging holes for a fence post and making repairs to a corral. Jake leaned up along a fence rail and greeted them. The men stopped what they were doing and looked over at him.

The older man stepped over and offered his hand. "Hello, I'm Aaron Kilbourne, and these are my two sons, Isaac and Jacob; what can I do for thee?" Jake shook the man's hand; the grip was so strong it almost broke his bones.

"I don't know if Rachel told you who I am, but I came out here today to see if your two sons would be willing to work for me for a couple of days." Aaron Kilbourne was as wise as his hair was grey; he would often remain silent and let others talk first.

"Father, I know who this man is," Jacob interrupted.

Aaron held up his hand for his younger son to be quiet. He looked at Jake and said, "Tell us who thou art."

After explaining to the men who he really was and why he was in town, Marshal Silver then turned to Isaac and Jacob and asked them if they would be willing to help. "I need more eyes around town to keep track of a couple of men. I also need someone I can trust; from what I've seen and heard about you, I believe you are the men for the job."

The two young men looked at each other and then Isaac said, "Marshal, we are peace loving people. We do not involve ourselves in fighting or gunplay. We certainly would not even consider shooting someone."

Silver shook his head understandingly. "I would not ask you to shoot anyone," he said, "Part of the reason I asked for your help is that no one would suspect you were helping me---regardless of whether they know who I am or not. Besides," he continued, "I would prefer to take these men alive and I need your help to do that."

The two considered it for a minute and conferred with each other. "If all ye need is our eyes, then we will help thee," Isaac said, "Capturing these men would be for the greater good...and perhaps we can save their souls afterwards."

Jacob then asked, "Who do you need us to watch?"

His father interrupted, "Let us sit to supper first and then we can discuss the details. Rachel has put on a good meal and I'm sure she will not mind the good marshal here joining us." He had a twinkle in his eye as he said that last part, and then he gestured for all to follow him over to the house.

When they walked into the house, Aaron Kilbourne asked his daughter to set another place at the table. She looked behind him to see Silver standing there with a grin on his face. Fire burned in her eyes for a moment before she remembered to be hospitable. "I suppose I'll not forget him as soon as I presumed," she thought.

As they sat down to eat, there was silence for several minutes. Rachel could not stand to sit quiet anymore and asked, "Father, why hast thou asked this man to join us for supper?"

With some mischievousness he answered simply, "All men need to eat, my daughter." She started to turn red in the face as her brothers were chuckling to themselves.

Jake intervened, "Miss Kilbourne, I must ask your forgiveness. I am not who you think I am."

"Really?" she replied, "Who are ye then?"

Jake took out his badge and placed it on the table for her to see. He then explained to her that he was using an alias and working undercover.

She looked at him while still not fully accepting his explanation. "And thy business with my brothers?" she asked.

Silver told her how he needed her brothers help.

She stood up angrily, "Why they could be killed!" she exclaimed. "This is not a good idea." Her younger brother Jacob tried to calm her down and told her that they would not be anywhere near any shooting, if it should occur. She was not satisfied and stormed out of the room.

Her father quietly said, "Do not worry thyself, she will soon come to see that this is good. Rachel has always been a spirited girl and quick to judgment."

Jake stood up to leave, "Thank you for supper and for your help; it's getting late so I should be getting back." He looked at the brothers, "If you two can meet me tomorrow in town, we can work out our strategy." They agreed and he walked out to get his horse.

Rachel was sitting in a rocking chair on the front porch as he walked out. He looked at her for a moment before saying anything. She looked beautiful with the last streaks of light coming from the setting sun on her face. "Miss Kilbourne," he began, "I apologize again for misleading you before. I hope you understand that it was something that I had to do."

She looked over at him, her face and mood had softened. "I forgive thee Marshal Silver; I suppose thou workest in mysterious ways as well as the Lord."

He chuckled at her humor, "I suppose so. Perhaps now you would consider having dinner with me again? Tomorrow evening?"

She smiled at him, "Marshal, I do not think that would look right, given thine alter ego."

"Yes, I guess you're right about that." He just couldn't think straight around this woman. "Then we should have a picnic lunch out by the stream. How does that sound?"

She considered his proposal for a moment, "I accept thy offer Mister Silver. I will make our lunch; thou will pick me up precisely at noon."

Jake replied, "Yes ma'am," and with a bigger grin than ever, he swung up on his horse and rode back towards town.

Chapter Six

Jake Silver was standing in the middle of the street. It was dark from the storm clouds, and the rain was drizzling down. Down the street stood a man, tall and imposing, his hat pulled down low so you couldn't see his face. His rain slicker was pulled back behind his holster; his gun hung low, ready to be pulled at a moments notice.

Silver waited for the man to make the first move. He was soaking wet and shivering from the cold. The rain was hitting him in the face, making it hard to see. He dared not wipe the water away in case the other man took it as a sign to draw.

Suddenly, he saw the other man go for his gun; Jake reached down and with lightning speed he drew. His gun was heavy and he found it awkward to lift. Finally he got the gun up and fired, but the other man was suddenly too far away. His shot fell short; hitting the mud and splashing up water from where it landed. He could see the other man's bullet coming towards him, slow and straight. It landed square into his chest and exploded.

Jake awoke with a start. He was sweating but cold; he had left the window open and it was cold in the early autumn morning. He took a moment to get his wits about him. "Dreamin' again," he said, "I've got to stop this." He was annoyed with himself for these dreams that plagued him on a regular basis. They had started several years ago after he had nearly been shot in a gunfight. The other man had pulled first and got off the first shot. His gun had still been held down in his holster and he was unable to pull it. Luckily, the other man had missed and he pulled a .36 revolver from behind his belt and shot the man. Ever since then the dreams, in various forms, had started. Strangely, it was only while he was on an assignment that they plagued him. While that event had really shaken him, he had learned from his mistake and now was always ready in a fight. Perhaps the dreams were there to help keep him from forgetting. Either way, they were still annoying.

After getting up, Jake shaved and washed his face. He went down to the hotel office and smiled at a stranger behind the counter. "Who are you?" he asked the man.

The man, really just a boy, looked up and said, "I'm Caleb; I help Mister Blake when he is out."

"Oh," Jake replied, "I was wondering if I could use that buggy that you have out back this afternoon? I need to take a ride out into the country."

Caleb checked for any notes on the desk, "It should be all right, I'll let Mister Blake know you need it."

Silver walked out onto the street and looked around. The Kilbourne brothers would be in soon, and he wanted to be ready for them. He walked over to the restaurant for some breakfast and then headed to the saloon. Sitting down on the front porch, Jake waited for them to show. It was a lovely morning; the air was crisp and cool, the sun was starting to warm things up for the day, and large billowing clouds drifted slowly across the blue sky.

He didn't have to wait for long. Just a few minutes later, the two rode in on a couple of really nice horses; Isaac rode on a large buckskin and Jacob was riding a beautiful red dun. The horses were obviously well bred and well taken care of.

Silver stood up and greeted the two. "Why don't we meet around back and we'll work out what we need to do." They agreed and casually made their way behind the saloon. The building had several stacks of empty barrels which they used to hide behind. Anyone seeing the three of them talking might become suspicious.

After looking around, Jake sat down on a small crate and delivered his plan. "Isaac, I want you to keep an eye on Daniel O'Connell. Do you know who he is?"

"Yes," he replied simply.

Jake continued, "Try to find a place that is inconspicuous to watch the post office from across the street. Just watch his movements and let me know where he goes, and with whom he meets. And by all means, if he holds up the bank, come runnin'." They all chuckled and then he turned to Jacob. "I want you to keep an eye on William O'Connell. He is my main suspect. Do like I told your brother and just track his movements and report back to me."

"What will ye be doing?" Jacob asked.

"I still have to check out another suspect, plus I will work with the sheriff to take these men down as soon as they make their move."

"Do ye want us to start right now?" Isaac asked.

"No, the auction is on Friday and they will have to wait until afterwards when the bank is full of money. Just ride in tomorrow morning and take up your stations; get here early so as to make sure you keep them covered. With all the people that are in town now, I would not be able to watch all their movements."

They worked out a meeting point for sharing information, and then Silver thanked them again for the help. The two brothers got on their horses and rode off. Jake sat there for a few minutes to see if anyone had spotted them or was watching. Satisfied that all was well, he got up and walked back to the front of the saloon.

From his room behind the barn, Colin Machen, who had just rolled out of his cot, stretched and looked out of the small window that was above his bed. He saw Black come out from behind a stack of barrels and walk around to the street. Colin quickly dressed and headed out. He went over to the saloon and looked around behind the building. He didn't see anything suspicious or out of place, but he stood there scratching his head for a minute. He just couldn't figure out what this man was doing in town. His cousin did not seem at all worried, so shrugging his shoulders Colin went back to the barn. He was sick of shoveling manure and living in this stinkin' barn; if he could read and write better, he could have had the job at the post office instead of Daniel. He almost couldn't stand to wait any longer. Just a few more days and he could leave all this behind him.

Silver looked down the street; it was dusty as another herd of longhorns had just been moved into the stockyard. Men were setting up the stage for the auctioneer, getting ready for tomorrow, and the buyers were already checking out the livestock, planning for which of the animals they would bid on.

Walking around the bank, Jake looked at the building again, trying to figure out how the gang would get inside. There was no way that he could see from the street, so he would have to wait for them to make their move and catch them in the act.

Jake then moved over to the barn. So far the stable hand had kept out of sight, thwarting his efforts to check him out. He quietly slid the large door open a few feet and slipped inside. It was dark in the barn with the doors closed and he stood there waiting for his eyes to adjust to the dim light. He tried to listen for any signs of Colin, but there was too much noise from across the street. Silently he crept along the stalls towards the back of the barn. There was a door at the back of the barn so Silver walked up to it and tried the latch. Gently he pulled on the latch and pushed but the door would not open. "Must be locked from inside," he surmised.

There didn't seem to be anyone about so he went to the stall which held his horse and checked on it. The feeding trough was empty so he went over and picked up a bundle of hay, took it over, and placed it in the trough. He spoke a few words to the horse while he combed it down. Carefully he moved around the horse while watching to see if anyone was in the barn. After a few minutes, he left his horse and made his way out. Jake glanced around the corner of the building towards the blacksmith shop; there were a couple of cowboys getting their horses re-shoed but no one else was around.

"I'll have to try again later," he told himself. For now, he decided to sit across the street from the bank and just watch the world go by. Perhaps he would see his suspect and then he could go talk to him. He was sure this guy was part of the gang. He didn't have any real proof, just a gut feeling. Plus, he recalled that he spoke with an Irish accent the first time they had met. He would wait for a couple of hours and then he would have to go; he had a date with a lovely lady for lunch. Sitting there, he thought about Rachel. She was spirited and beautiful; he enjoyed watching her move around, hearing her voice... He stopped himself; he needed to pay attention to the task at hand. There would be time for her later.

Chapter Seven

Jake Silver had changed into a fresh suit, combed back his hair, and brushed off his hat. He checked his reflection in the small mirror above the washstand. "I guess that'll do," he thought. He walked down the stairs to find Mr. Blake behind the desk. "Do you have that buggy ready for me?" he growled at the man.

"Yes sir," Blake said as his shaking hand took the key. "Caleb should have the horse hitched up and ready for you."

"Thanks," Silver said with a smile; he decided to be nicer to this man from now on. He walked out the front door and found the buggy ready to go. Climbing onto the rig, he snapped the reins against the horse and rode off out of town.

Samuel Blake watched the man ride off as he ran his fingers through his thinning hair. He could not believe what he had just heard. "My prayers must be working," he said to himself. Encouraged, he decided he was going to pray some more and maybe God would give him the strength to work up the nerve to preach to that man.

A mile west of town, Rachel Kilbourne was fussing about the house. She had kicked everyone out of the kitchen so she could prepare the lunch basket. Her younger brother, Jacob, had been teasing her about her date and the way she was reacting to it. She was annoyed with herself for acting this way, but she wanted everything to be perfect.

Her father stood in the doorway watching her for a while. "Do ye think ye are being foolish?" he asked her.

Rachel was startled to find he had been watching her. "I am just trying to get everything ready; he will be here any minute."

Aaron Kilbourne sympathized with his daughter, he knew what she was feeling but he wanted her to relax and enjoy the day instead of worrying. "Ye are like Martha, in Luke, chapter ten, all busy with the unimportant preparations when Jesus came to visit. Ye should be like her sister, Mary, who was focused on the relationship. That Marshal Silver likes thee," Aaron continued, "As long as he is with thee, he won't care one wit about the food and those little doilies ye are packing."

Rachel stopped for a moment and looked at her father. "Ye are right of course, but I don't care right now. Get out of my kitchen and go watch for him to arrive." With that she shooed him out and returned to her preparations.

Silver rode up to the house a few minutes later. Aaron was sitting on the front step watching him arrive. He stepped out and greeted the Marshal, "Rachel should be ready; I'll go get her."

"Thanks," Jake replied. He stood there unsure of what to do with himself. He felt like a schoolboy with a crush on the girl sitting next to him. He told himself to stop acting like an idiot. "It's not like this is the first girl to whom you've ever talked," he said to himself. Jake took off his hat and smoothed out his hair, waiting for her to come out.

Suddenly, the door opened and Rachel was standing there. Jake took a moment and gazed at this woman in front of him. She had her hair pulled up, revealing a long, slim neck, and wore a plain straw hat, perfect for a picnic in the countryside. She wore a long riding skirt and a plain white blouse.

Jake stepped forward to take the picnic basket from her and offered her his arm. "You look very nice today," he said. She simply smiled and they walked over to the rig. He helped her up and then placed the basket behind the seat.

They rode about a mile or two westward, toward the foothills and the stream that came out from the mountains in the distance. Not much was said on the ride, but they simply enjoyed each others company. As they arrived at the small stream, Jake slowed the horse and crossed over to the other side. There was a small grassy area with some cottonwood trees along the water.

They got down and spread out a blanket. Sitting down, Jake watched her unpack the basket. She had cold roasted chicken, potato salad, and bread. Rachel laid out some plates and homemade napkins along with silverware. Next she pulled out a jar with apple cider and poured out the drinks.

Jake looked over the spread and said, "This all looks great, I can't wait to dig in."

Rachel told him to wait. "First we must give thanks to the Lord for His bounty." Jake feigned being impatient with a sigh, but he folded his hands and gave the blessing for the food.

Rachel took the plates and served the food. Occasionally, she would glance at this man who sat quietly and watched her. She gave a slight smile as she realized that her father had been right. It was a joy just to be with someone, everything else didn't matter.

They ate without saying much to each other. The gurgling of the water and the singing of the birds in the trees filled the air. As he finished, Jake complimented her on the food. "Everything was wonderful; the chicken was better than what they serve at the restaurant."

"Thank you," she replied, "I'm glad ye enjoyed it. I also have some apple pie for dessert, but I think we should wait before having any; I'm full right now." Jake agreed and they walked over to the stream to sit on a large boulder next to the water.

They sat there watching the water roll and swirl around the rocks. A dragonfly flirted around the two, and then perched on a branch overhanging a small pool. They made small talk for a while and then the conversation turned more personal. Rachel asked him about his job, his past, and what he wanted for the future.

After explaining to her about his life as a young man, he spent several minutes talking about his time in the Civil War. "I was a skirmisher, taking pot shots at officers on the other side. If we could take out an officer, the soldiers would be confused for a while allowing our troops to advance with limited causalities."

"Did ye enjoy doing that?" Rachel asked.

"I did," Jake answered. "It was exciting work for a young kid, although I did get sick a couple of times after seeing all the killing.

"After the war, I decided to join the Marshals Service. I was still young and seeking adventure and excitement and the west seemed like the place to go, so here I am."

"And what about the future?" Rachel queried.

"I suppose I'll settle down sometime soon," Jake surmised, "There just always seems to be one more job that needs to be done. I would like to have a horse ranch someday and breed thoroughbreds."

"That sounds nice," she said quietly, thinking to herself that she could be part of that.

Tired of talking about himself, Jake asked her about growing up in Pennsylvania and being a Quaker.

"We try to live a quiet, peaceful, and simple life," she said, "We believe in God and read the Bible just like other Christians; I think the only difference is in our worship service."

Jake asked, "What is different?"

"We sit quietly until someone receives a word from the Lord, and then they will share it with everyone. We usually do not have a preacher such as ye are familiar with."

"I understand all that," Jake said, "But why do you use 'thee' and 'thou' when you talk? That sort of language went out of style a hundred years ago."

Rachel laughed, "Well, I suppose it is old fashioned, but it is the language of the Bible so we feel it is good enough to keep using it."

Curious, Jake asked her about her future.

Suddenly shy, Rachel just said, "I am waiting for the right man to show up in my life."

Getting up from the rock they had been sitting on, they strolled down along the stream. The afternoon had turned warm from the clear, sunny day but the coolness of the shade under the trees along the banks of the stream was refreshing. Jake hardly noticed the weather as he was watching this girl walking next to him; however, she looked like she was concerned about something.

"What are you thinking about?" he asked.

Pausing for a moment before turning towards him, Rachel said, "I'm worried about my brothers helping you tomorrow, especially Jacob. He is still young and impulsive, I'm afraid that something bad will happen."

Jake took her hands in his and looked into her eyes, "There is nothing to worry about; all they are going to be doing is watching and reporting back to me. They will not be anywhere near any kind of danger. Besides, I'm paying them each ten dollars a day to help me." He immediately regretted saying that last part.

Rachel's eyes lit on fire and she angrily shot out, "I don't care about the money! Don't ye understand? This is not the sort of activity in which they should be involved." She pulled her hands away and turned to walk back. Jake looked after her thinking about what she said.

He ran up to her and spoke softly, "You are like a mother to those boys, aren't you?"

She looked up at him, having calmed down a little and said, "Yes, ever since our mother died I have helped to raise them, especially Jacob, he was still so young at the time."

Jake led her back to the blanket and they sat down. "Well, I promise you that I will not let anything happen to them. If it comes to any shooting the sheriff and I can handle things." Trying to lighten the mood, he added, "You could worry about me, Friend Rachel, if you want."

Smiling, Rachel said, "Marshal Silver, I believe ye can handle thyself just fine, but I'll pray for thee just the same."

"That sounds good to me," he replied, "Now how about some of that pie that you made?"

Chapter Eight

When Jake and Rachel had finished their dessert, it was getting late. They got back in the buggy and rode back to the Kilbourne farm. The sun was low in the sky, the shadows long across the land. Jake pulled up the buggy at the front porch of the house and got down. He walked around and helped Rachel out. "I hope that I didn't upset you too much earlier," he began.

"No," she replied, "I do realize that ye need help tomorrow and ye needed someone ye could trust; however, I still am worried about them…and thee, a little." She smiled slightly and he grinned back at her.

"You are right about one thing," he stated, "I can handle myself and I'll handle this gang tomorrow. You have nothing to worry about." With that he took her arm and led her up to the door. Had this been just any girl, he would have planted a kiss on her and walked away. But Rachel was special, well he thought about kissing her anyway, but he just squeezed her hand and said goodnight. He respected her and her moral values so he had to control his urges. She returned his goodbye and went inside, watching through the window as he rode off.

Returning back to town, Jake put the buggy away just as it had turned dark. Since it was too early for bed he went over to the saloon to pass the time. He sat at the bar with a glass of beer, watching and listening to the conversations around him. The room was full with all the extra people in town. Some of the cowboys were playing poker, trying to increase their meager wages. Several of the ranchers were discussing cattle prices and trying to predict how much they could bring in at the auction tomorrow. At the far wall, a man who was very drunk was trying to play the piano. A bar maid was trying to sing along and it all made for quite a racket. Two men, who had had enough, took the drunk by each arm and threw him out of the saloon and into the street.

The double batwing doors were still swinging when the sheriff walked in. He looked around the room, occasionally greeting people that he knew. When he saw Silver, he made his way over. Jake greeted him with a nod and turned back to his drink. Sheriff Murphy ordered a drink of his own and downed half of the glass before speaking.

The sheriff kept his face forward so that no one would see him talking to the man they knew as Black. "How is everything going?" he asked.

"Fine," Silver replied. The marshal quickly filled in the sheriff about his suspects and his plan for tomorrow.

"What do you need me to do?" the sheriff asked.

"Just do your normal job and keep an eye on things. Just don't go near the bank, I don't want that gang getting spooked and canceling their plans. I'll come get you when I need you."

With that, Jake finished his drink and headed out. He went back over to the hotel to turn in for the night. As he walked in, Samuel Blake handed him his key. Samuel's hand was not shaking for the first time since he had met this man. Jake took the key and chuckled to himself as he went up the stairs to his room. "Maybe I won't have to apologize to him after all," he said to himself. He got ready for bed and thought about Rachel as he lay down to sleep. He was going to have to decide what to do about her when this affair was over. "She is quite a woman," he thought as he drifted off to sleep.

An hour later, Daniel O'Connell climbed up onto the roof of the Mercantile. The false front of the building offered him the perfect cover. He sat on the roof and perched his rifle across the facade of the building. It was a moonless night so he was hidden from sight; anyone who by chance happened to look up would not be able to see him. The lights from the buildings and a couple of bonfires in the street allowed him to see just fine. From this vantage point, he could see up the street to the bank and all the way down to the sheriff's office. It should only be a short time before his brother and cousin began their work. His stomach gave him a small cramp just like always, but he ignored it.

From his room behind the barn, Colin changed into some dark clothing and then slipped out unseen. He made his way the short distance to the back of the watch shop. When he reached the door, he looked around quickly and seeing no one he turned the doorknob and went inside.

William was sitting at his workbench putting some tools into a small satchel. "Are you ready?" he simply asked his cousin.

"Yes," Colin replied, "Is Daniel in place?"

"Aye, me lad," William said, slipping into his full Irish accent. He was almost giddy with the thought of what they were about to do. After everything had settled down in town he could make his getaway. Colin was going to leave on Sunday along with most of the outsiders; hopefully without anyone in town noticing. Daniel would leave sometime next week, and then he would follow a short time later. They had made arrangements to meet at a hotel in Denver and from there to California.

He finished putting together his supplies and grinning up at Colin said, "Let's go." They went upstairs to the bedroom where the gear was waiting. A small ladder led up to the trapdoor; Colin went up the ladder, opened the trapdoor and stepped out onto the roof. From below, William handed up the poles and tackle along with the rope. With everything in place, they took the boards, which they had stashed along the roof edge earlier, and slid them across the space to the bank roof. The bank was slightly lower but not too much to be a problem. They had nailed a small piece of wood across the board, a foot from the end, to keep it from sliding.

William then strapped the poles to Colin's back and he crawled slowly across. The boards held in place, only bending slightly, so William grabbed the tackle and walked across. They returned to retrieve the tools and the length of rope, and then went back across to the bank roof.

Due to the lack of windows in the bank, the builders had installed skylight windows in the roof to let light in. For whatever reason, no one ever suspected that thieves would try to get in that way. William, however, the first time he stepped foot in the bank, thought of it. The second day they were in town and had decided to stay, William went into the bank to open an account and case out the place. He had almost laughed out loud when he looked up and saw the skylights. The fact that the business next door to the bank was for sale was almost too good to believe. All they needed next was a diversion, like a big cattle auction, to take everyone's attention away from their activities.

Planning this job had taken longer than most; his discreet questions to the bank owner, Paul Schmidt, proved unsuccessful. The man would not discuss the bank's security in any detail except to say that the bank would never be successfully robbed. He apparently had a new type of safe that no one had ever cracked. "We'll just see about that," William thought.

Colin was setting up the block and tackle at the peak of three poles which had been lashed together. They would use this arrangement for William to lower himself down to the bank floor. Meanwhile, William was using a pry bar to pull up the window along the frame. If they could avoid damaging it, no one would know how they had gotten in.

When they had removed the window, they carried over the tripod and positioned it above the opening.

William put the satchel of tools and supplies over his shoulder and put the hook from the tackle into his belt. He lowered himself down to the floor and unhooked himself. From above, Colin pulled the hook back up and then lowered himself down. They took out a small lantern and lit it. Looking around, there was an office with a locked door, another desk along the back wall, several locked cabinets behind the teller's window, and the safe. William looked at it for several minutes; it had been surrounded with brick, two blocks thick. He had never seen anything like it, although he had heard about something like this. "I guess the rumors were true," he said to himself, "This is going to be a challenge."

Across the street, Daniel was starting to sweat even though the night air was cool. He had been sitting there for two long hours and still no movement. "What is taking them so long?" he wondered. Down on the street, some people still wandered around, mostly going home after a night at the saloon.

Next, he noticed the sheriff come out of the saloon. He looked up and down the street before heading up towards the bank. Daniel watched the man, holding him in his gun sights. His rifle slowly moved along as the man strolled from building to building. As the sheriff stopped briefly in front of the bank, Daniel held his breath and put his finger on the trigger. But then the sheriff moved on; crossing the street and making his way back down the other side. The sniper breathed a sigh of relief as he watched him walk to the jailhouse and go inside.

Inside the bank, the two men had finished their work and hoisted themselves back up to the roof. They disassembled the tripod, put the window back in place, and carried their gear back across to the other building. They used the rope to lower the long boards to the ground, and then brought all the other gear inside with them.

"Did you have to do that?" Colin asked, "It took forever."

William just smiled and said, "Don't worry about it. Let's get the tackle and those boards and hide them behind the barn before anyone sees them."

From the roof of the Mercantile, Daniel watched as his partners grabbed the boards from where they had lain and took them around behind the barn. He then got up and stretched his legs, and made his way off the roof and around to the back door of his brother's shop. When William and Colin returned they went inside.

"What took so long?" Daniel asked.

Colin shook his head, "I'll tell you later."

William lit a candle at the table and sat down. "Everything went according to plan. Just go about your business for the next few days and act normal. You know the plan; we leave town separately over the next couple of weeks and meet up in Denver. However, pack your bags now just in case something goes wrong and we have to leave suddenly." He paused, going over things in his mind, "And no contact with each other unless absolutely necessary."

They shook hands and congratulated each other on a job well done. Colin and Daniel waited until William doused the light and then they left the room, sneaking back to their own homes.

Chapter Nine

Friday morning started early in South Plains. This was the biggest day of the year. Cattle had been brought in from two dozen different ranches, cattle buyers and auctioneers were getting ready for the day, business owners were open early to be ready for all the customers they hoped would come in. The cowboys were the only ones getting up late. They would have to be ready later to move the cattle to the railroad after the sales took place. Besides, most of them had drunk too much the night before and needed the sleep.

William O'Connell was up early as well. He did not open his shop because he didn't care if he did any business today or any day for that matter. The excitement was just too great to sleep. He put on his best frock coat suit with a low cut vest and a small tied cravat. Then he oiled back his hair and slipped on his best derby hat with a small, colorful duck feather stuck in the band.

William walked out the front door of his shop and locked the door behind him. After having some breakfast at the restaurant he planned to enjoy the proceedings of the day. He also wanted to make sure that the townsfolk saw him around just in case there were questions.

As William walked up the step to the restaurant, Jacob Kilbourne looked at the ground, keeping his head down. He had been sitting on the walkway in front of the building, keeping an eye on his target.

After the man went inside, he pulled out a small notebook from inside his coat, made a few notations, and put it away again. Jacob then sat and waited for the man to finish his meal.

Marshal Jake Silver was also up early. He had gotten dressed while it was still dark and headed over to the stables. Just as the first streams of light showed from the rising sun, Silver slid open the barn door and went inside. He had taken just two steps when Colin Machen popped his head up from behind a stall. Colin had been preparing a horse for riding when he heard the door open.

With no place to hide, he put on a smile and greeted Silver, "What can I do for ya this fine mornin'?"

Silver glared at the man, "Nothing, just getting my horse, and I'll do it myself."

Colin lost his smile and turned away to finish what he was doing. "I really hate that man," he thought, "But after tomorrow I won't have to deal with him anymore."

Silver led his horse out of the stables and tied it up in front of the hotel. He wanted it ready to ride at a moment's notice, if needed. After making sure all his gear was ready, he went over to the corrals where he could watch the crowds and also keep an eye on the stables and the bank. He also was ready to act at a moment's notice.

Isaac Kilbourne was bored. He had been sitting in front of the sheriff's office for four hours now. There had been absolutely no movement from inside the post office. Several people had gone in to do business, but Daniel O'Connell had not come out or even shown his face. Isaac was getting sleepy so he forced himself to get up and walk around.

After pacing back and forth a few times, he saw Sheriff Murphy coming towards him. The sheriff stopped and asked him how it was going.

"I'm bored to tears here Sheriff," he said, "I sure hope Jacob is having more fun than I am."

Murphy chuckled, "Well, come on in and have a cup of coffee, maybe that'll help keep you awake."

Isaac went inside with the sheriff. They discussed the situation while enjoying the coffee. "Do ye really think the bank will be robbed today like the marshal says?" Isaac asked.

"I don't," the sheriff replied, "But the marshal is absolutely convinced that it will. I suppose we'll just have to trust him on it."

"I suppose." Isaac had been watching out of the window at the building across the street. "What do ye think he will do if the bank isn't robbed today?"

Murphy rubbed his chin while thinking of an answer, "I don't know; perhaps we'll have to keep an eye on them again tomorrow."

Isaac groaned, "I don't think I could do this for another day."

He walked back outside to take up his post while the sheriff laughed to himself. He did not envy Isaac's job today; at least he could walk around town as he wished.

The auction was well under way; the air was dusty as cattle were being moved around from pen to pen. It was getting hot as the sun climbed higher in the sky and a hundred people or so were gathered around. The auctioneer was calling for a higher bid, trying to get as much money as he could out of the buyers. Selling low now would keep prices low all day. It was a juggling act between buyers and sellers, all trying to get a good bargain.

Silver was getting hot. Taking off his hat, he wiped the sweat from his brow and took yet another look around. He kept his back to the activities of the auction and watched the town. The bank was busy; as transactions at the auction were completed the money was rushed over to be deposited. Occasionally, he saw the stable hand come out, taking care of a customer, but he never left the premises of the barn.

Silver turned to look over the crowd. As his eyes passed over the rows of people he saw William O'Connell looking straight at him. The man had a big smile on his face as he turned away to watch the proceedings. One lot of fat longhorns had just gone for a record price and the crowd cheered. As Silver watched William, the man looked over again. The smile never left his face. Jake frowned as he turned back towards the town; something was wrong or out of place, he just didn't know what it was.

As the day wore on, the thought kept nagging at him that he had misjudged something. The gang was most likely going to strike later, after the bank had closed. He had not told his two helpers this as he wanted them to stay ready for anything that might occur. He decided to go get something to eat. There would not be time to eat later if his suspicions were correct.

Jake turned to go and bumped into a young man standing there. "Pardon me," Silver said as he passed the man. The man lifted his head and looked at Silver for a moment before pulling his hat down low on his face again. As Jake walked away he realized it had been Jacob---he had been wearing a false, drooping mustache as a disguise!

Silver turned back around and said, "Take that thing off, you look ridiculous." He laughed as he walked away, heading towards the restaurant.

As the afternoon wore on, the auction wore down. There were only a few lots left to auction off and the crowds were thinning out. William O'Connell had stayed at the auction for most of the day but now headed over to the saloon. Jacob kept a close eye on him, noting where he went and when, always maintaining a good cover.

Daniel O'Connell stayed in the post office all day, not even coming out for lunch. Isaac was going out of his mind; he felt like he was wasting time, he had been raised to never be idle. He consoled himself by reminding himself that he was getting paid and this was a job.

Colin Machen finally left the barn just before dinner. Silver watched him from a distance as he went over to the tailor shop and disappeared inside. Jake casually strolled over and glanced in the window as he walked by. The tailor was showing Colin a new suit, holding it ready for him to try it on. Jake went around the corner of the building and waited. After several minutes, Colin came out with a bundle under his arm and carrying a new suitcase. After watching him return to his room behind the barn, Silver went inside the tailor shop.

The tailor, Paul Morton, was glad to see him; two customers in the same day! He was going to make some money today. "How can I help you, sir? These are the newest fashions from New York." He held up two jackets for him to see.

Silver held up his badge for Morton to see. "I'm a deputy marshal and I want you to tell me everything your last customer said to you."

Suddenly the tailor was not so happy, but maybe he could still make a sale. "Yes sir," he began, "That young Colin said he was taking a trip and needed a new suit---bought a new suitcase as well."

"Did he say when or where he was going?" Jake asked.

Morton thought for a moment, "No, just that he was leaving on the next train.

"Now, how about you sir, that jacket you are wearing has seen a few miles; how about a new one?"

"Not today," Jake said, and then pointing at the man he continued, "And don't tell anyone you talked to me."

Morton held up his hands in surrender, "No sir," he said to Silver's back as he was walking out the door.

Now convinced that he was right about every-thing, Jake went over to relieve Isaac. "Go get something to eat and be ready to keep an eye out for the entire night," he told him. After Isaac returned he did the same for Jacob. Each brother had given him an update on the day's activities. "Poor Isaac," he thought, "Must have been a long day for him. Maybe tonight's activities will offer him some excitement."

Touching base with Sheriff Murphy he reminded him, "Stay out of sight tonight, I don't want them to postpone their plans." He also told the sheriff to hang out in the saloon so he would be close by when needed.

Next, he got his horse and took it over to the freight office which was across from the bank. He could hide behind some crates that were piled up beside the building and wait for the bandits to make their move.

As it started to get dark, a small sliver of the moon rose over the horizon. One by one, stars started to appear and the cool night air crept in. Along the street, several bonfires were lit to help illuminate things for those who stayed up late. There was plenty of revelry over at the saloon, both satisfied ranchers who had made some money and cattle buyers who had plenty of stock to take back to the cities.

As Jake Silver sat waiting, he could hear all the sounds from down the street drifting over to where he was hiding. Other than the occasional drunk singing as he stumbled home, there was no movement outside. Watching the bank closely as well as the shop next door, he changed position again as his legs grew stiff, trying to keep them limber for when action was needed.

Two doors down, next to the Mercantile, Jacob was nodding off to sleep. He had taken up position along the alleyway between the restaurant and the mercantile. After a long day, he was now bored and too comfortable, lying up against the building, to keep his eyes open.

Down at the other end of the street, Isaac was munching on some jerky that he had brought along, and sipping some coffee that the sheriff had provided for him. The light inside the back room of the post office where Daniel stayed had turned off an hour earlier. There had been no movement since; it appeared that the man was sound asleep, which was exactly what Isaac wanted to do as well.

Minutes dragged into hours and Jake was starting to get concerned. It was now well after midnight and nothing had happened. He rose from his position and snuck around the backside of the buildings to where Jacob was hiding. The young man was sound asleep so Silver kicked him awake. "I guess you haven't seen anything?" he asked.

Jacob, yawning and stretching, apologized, "I'm sorry Marshal, I just couldn't keep my eyes open." Silver understood and told him to watch out while he went over to check on Isaac.

With the cool air of the night and the coffee, Isaac was awake and alert. He saw the marshal coming over and stood up to greet him. "Is something happening?" he asked.

"No, I just wanted to check with you to see if you have seen anything." Isaac told him that all was quiet.

"Alright, stick with it, I'll check on you again at first light if nothing happens before that."

Silver went back to his spot behind the crates to wait out the night. The minutes ticked by slowly. He detected no movement and the only sound he heard were some coyotes howling off in the distance.

Chapter Ten

Dawn broke gradually as the sun slowly rose across the eastern plains. Jake Silver sat behind the shipping crates, thinking. He had had plenty of time to think over these past few hours. What had gone wrong? Were they foolish enough to wait another day to make their move? That didn't seem likely as much of the extra money would be sent out the next day on the train to Denver. Did they make a move and he just didn't see it somehow? That was the only scenario which he could imagine. "So what to do next?" he asked himself. He was still thinking when he got up to check on the Kilbourne brothers.

As he walked over he decided the only course was to raid the O'Connell shop and see what was what. Silver told Jacob to continue to keep watch while he went to confer with the sheriff. Isaac was still on watch and reported that he had seen nothing. They both went inside to meet with the sheriff.

"The first thing we need to do is check the bank." Silver stated. "Sheriff, you go get Schmidt and we'll meet you over there."

Walking back, Jake was furious with himself; he couldn't believe that he had been outsmarted by this group. He reached into his vest pocket and took out his badge. He slipped it on, over his heart, for all to see. Next he reached down and checked his gun. He knew it was loaded and ready, but he double checked it anyway.

As they reached the bank, Sheriff Murphy and Paul Schmidt ran over to meet them. The banker was still trying to put his tie in place as they arrived. "Do you think my bank was robbed?" he asked incredulously.

"I'm sure something happened, I just don't know what. Now open this door and we'll check."

Paul unlocked the door and opened it slowly. Peering inside he didn't see anything out of place. Silver motioned for the Kilbourne brothers to stay outside and he pulled his pistol and went in, followed by the sheriff.

They walked around slowly, looking at everything. Schmidt unlocked the door to access the teller's counter. All the drawers and cabinets were locked and nothing was out of place. Next he unlocked the door to the back room. Silver threw the door open and looked around quickly, ready for anything.

They were quiet for a moment, looking around. There was no indication that any bank robbery had occurred. Silver stood looking at the safe. It was odd looking; like nothing he had ever seen before. Schmidt stood next to him smiling.

"It's a Corliss cannonball safe," he said proudly.

Jake looked at the man, "I've heard of these, but I've never seen one."

"Yes," the banker said, "It is a fairly new invention. They are round, like a cannonball, to prevent explosives from being able to blow it open. Also, it is extremely heavy; this one weighs in at around four thousand pounds so no one is going to just walk off with it."

"Well," Jake said, "Let's open it anyway---just to check."

The banker said "Alright," and bent down to open the safe. He spun the dial a few times and then rotated it back and forth dialing in the combination. Swinging open the heavy door revealed another lock on the inside.

Glancing back at the men he smiled proudly again and said, "You see? Another lock; no one can get into this safe." He unlocked the inside door and opened it as well. Inside the safe were piles of money. Paul quickly ran his fingers up and down the stacks of bills, quickly counting it.

"It's all here, Marshal; nothing is missing."

Silver stood there thinking for a minute before turning to the sheriff, "I know they did something, let's go next door and search O'Connell's place."

Sheriff Murphy held up his hand, "Now wait a minute, Marshal, we can't just burst in there; we have to have just cause." Jake looked at the man impatiently, "We do, let's go."

With that he stormed out of the bank to find a small crowd had gathered outside. Word had quickly spread that a robbery had occurred, and the even more exciting news that this man that everyone thought was up to no good was actually a U.S. Marshal. Many looked and pointed when they saw his badge and started shouting questions. Silver ignored them and started over to the shop next door.

Rachel Kilbourne was there and ran up to him. "Did they rob the bank? Did anyone get hurt?" she asked.

"I don't know anything yet; now let me do my job." She was sort of hurt by his short answer but she waited in the street.

Silver and Murphy climbed the step to the front door of the watchmakers shop. Jake pounded on the door until William O'Connell angrily opened it.

"What is it?" he shouted, but when he saw the badge on Silver's jacket his eyes went wide with shock. He quickly regained his composure and then his eyes narrowed with suspicion. "What do you want?" he asked again.

"I am Marshal Jake Silver and we would like to search your place."

Inside, William was kicking himself for not acting on his earlier suspicions about this man. Colin had warned him several times and he had just brushed it off.

"I think not," he said, staring defiantly at Silver.

Jake placed his hand on his gun and said, "If you are innocent then you have nothing to hide."

"Innocent of what?" William replied.

"Bank robbery," Silver said shortly, "Now let us in or I'll arrest you on suspicion."

William was trying to think quickly about how to handle this situation but then he had nothing to hide, so he let the men inside.

Outside, the crowd was murmuring among themselves, wondering what was going on. Near the back of the gathering, Daniel O'Connell quietly turned and headed back to his room. He quickly gathered his bag and his rifle, saddled up his horse and rode out from behind the town towards the railroad depot.

Inside the shop, they searched the building from top to bottom. Aside from the normal things found in a residence, there was nothing to indicate any wrongdoing. In the workshop, Jake was rooting around through the tools he found in a bag. While some of the tools could be used for breaking into a locked building, there was nothing unusual for a watchmaker or gunsmith to have. He met the sheriff back at the front door.

William had a smirk on his face, "Find what you were looking for?" he asked sarcastically. Jake ignored him and they walked out onto the board walkway.

Just then the banker ran up to him, waving some booklets in his hand. He had stayed in the bank when the others had left; even though he was sure that no one could possibly steal anything from his bank, he felt responsible to his customers to make sure. He had opened the cash drawers under the teller's counter checking for any issues, then he opened the locked cabinets where the books were kept. Something didn't look right when he pulled out the master ledger---the numbered pages were not in order. All the entries looked right, but the pages had definitely been tampered with. He then found the individual deposit booklet for William O'Connell, since he seemed to be a suspect, and looked at the totals. It was all wrong. While he couldn't remember the exact amount, Paul Schmidt prided himself for knowing generally how much money everyone had. After all, one had to know one's place in social circles. The total deposited amount in O'Connell's account was supposed to be around five thousand; the amount that now showed was over fifty thousand.

He ran up to the Marshal and handed him the booklets, he had grabbed the others that the marshal had suspected and they were off as well. Silver quickly looked at the books and realized what had happened. Instead of stealing the money in the safe, they had just forged the books and replaced them with the real ones. That way they could simply withdraw the money at a later date with the appearance of being completely legal.

He turned to look back at William just as the man slammed the door shut. Jake pulled his gun right before a shot rang out from beside the bank. Colin had been watching and waiting to see what had happened. When his cousin turned to flee, he shot towards the crowd to allow William time to escape.

When the shot rang out, the crowd screamed and everyone ran for cover. Silver quickly shot back towards Colin but he had disappeared behind the building. Jake shouted at the sheriff to go after William while he would get Colin.

Silver ran between the watch shop and the bank to try to cut Colin off before he reached the barn. He was halfway to the stables when Colin came racing out on a horse. Colin still had his gun out and shot towards Silver as he rode by. Jake dove to the ground and rolled as he hit the dirt. The shot had missed but Colin was off at a full gallop heading east out of town. Jake shot at the fleeing man but he was riding low in the saddle and quickly rode out of range. Silver then jumped up and ran back over to where he had left his horse to give chase.

Chapter Eleven

Sheriff Murphy kicked in the front door to the shop and dove inside. He had his gun drawn, ready for anything. He should have realized earlier that bursting into a gunsmiths shop wasn't a good idea. William was waiting for him, crouching behind a cabinet, holding a double barreled shotgun. He let loose with both barrels just after the sheriff came in. Since Murphy had dived to the floor the shot was off the mark, but he still managed to hit the sheriff in his arm; the arm which he used to shoot. The rest of the blast had taken out the front door and shattered the window that was next to it.

Sheriff Murphy was dazed for a moment after being hit. He had dropped his gun and was clutching his arm. When he looked up, William had already left. He picked up his revolver with his left hand and struggled to get up and chase after the man.

Meanwhile, William had raced back to the workshop and grabbed his bag. He snatched up his Colt which had been placed next to his bag and headed out the back door. He couldn't believe everything had fallen apart at the last second. All his plans were ruined by this marshal that had snuck into town.

William burst out of the door looking around; he needed a horse and fast. He hoped Colin had left one for him in the barn. As he started to run over, Jacob Kilbourne rode up on his red dun. He shouted out that he had found William hoping that someone would hear him.

William raised his gun and yelled, "Get off that horse!"

"No sir," Jacob replied, "The sheriff will be out here soon so ye had better give thyself up."

William wasn't going to wait, so he grabbed the horse and swung himself up behind Jacob. He held the gun to the young man's head and told him to ride off. Jacob froze, not knowing what to do. William kicked the horse into action and headed out of town towards the railroad.

Just then, Sheriff Murphy stumbled out of the door and tried to fire. He just couldn't hold his gun steady with his left hand; he also didn't want to hit the boy. He collapsed to the ground and looked at his bleeding arm. It was punctured with several pellets of birdshot; the blood was pouring down his arm so he pulled off his bandana and wrapped it around his arm.

Marshal Silver had just gotten to his horse when he heard a scream. He turned to see Rachel pointing towards the end of town. William was galloping off on the same horse as Jacob, holding a gun to his head. Silver reached for his Sharp's rifle; he could hit him as long as they rode steady.

Just as he was sighting down the gun, Rachel rode past on her black Morgan. The horse was small but fast and powerfully built. She kicked the horse into a full gallop, hysterical with fear for her little brother. Jake quickly pulled up his rifle to keep from hitting her. As soon as he realized what she was doing he shouted at her to stop. "Damn woman, what does she think she's going to do?"

He shoved the rifle back into its scabbard and swung up onto his horse to give chase. He spurred his horse into action, chasing Rachel who was chasing her brother. Silver soon realized that he was not going to catch up. Even though his Tennessee Pacer was able to run non-stop all day, it was not fast. The Morgan that Rachel was riding was perhaps the fastest horse in the whole town. All that Jake could hope for at this point was to take control of the situation when they all reached the train depot.

Two miles away, the train finished hooking all the cattle cars to the Baldwin 4-4-0 locomotive. Two passenger cars, a freight car, and a secure mail and baggage car were all ready to go. The locomotive clunked and hissed, seemingly alive; the steam pressure was fully built up and needed somewhere to go. The engineer blew the whistle, signaling the all aboard.

Just behind the depot, the sniper, Daniel O'Connell lay across the top of the water tank. At that level, he had a good view down the trail towards town. He had seen Colin ride up and board the train, and now he could see a dust trail off in the distance, indicating someone else was coming.

He held his Spencer rifle at the ready, looking down across the sights at the rider heading his way. As the rider drew closer, he could see it was William riding behind someone else. He was about to climb down when William rode up and saw him.

"Shoot them!" he yelled, pointing down the trail. William jumped off the horse and then swatted it on its rump, sending it running down the track.

On the water tower, Daniel lay back down and sighted down his rifle again. There were two riders coming, the first one was just in range and he took aim and fired. The bullet took one second to travel the three hundred yards, hitting the target square in the chest. As the rider fell off, her bonnet came off revealing her long, blond hair. Daniel could not believe it---he had just shot a woman! Sitting up, he was wondering what to do when he remembered there was another rider. He quickly cycled the lever of his rifle and pulled back the hammer. From a sitting position, he took aim and fired. The man, it looked like that marshal, was too far away; at five hundred yards the bullet landed short, hitting the dirt, kicking up a puff of dust.

When Jake saw Rachel fly off her horse, he swore loudly and was about to ride up to meet her. Just then he saw the bullet hit the ground in front of him. He pulled his horse up and jumped off. Realizing that one of the gang members was shooting at them, Silver pulled his Sharp's rifle out of the scabbard and laid it across the saddle of his horse to keep it steady.

On top of the water tower, Daniel knew he was out of range but he tried again. He raised the barrel of the gun up, far above where the sights aligned, trying to get the distance he needed. If nothing else, he would keep Silver away while they got away on the train. He pulled the trigger and waited for the shot to land. It was still off; he· had missed by over fifty yards.

Watching the area around the train depot, Jake saw the puff of smoke from atop the water tank.

"So that's where you're hiding, you bastard!"

Silver was furious that Rachel had been shot, angry with himself for letting her ride out ahead of him, and his rage was boiling. He had to take several breaths to steady himself; he took aim at the figure on top of the tower and fired. The Sharp's had a greater range than the Spencer, plus his gun had a longer, custom length barrel to increase its range. The rifle kicked and the bullet exploded out of the barrel. It took almost two seconds to travel the distance and slammed into Daniel's head, killing him instantly. The limp body rolled off the water tower and dropped the thirty feet to the ground.

William watched his brother die. He stared at the body, which had dropped right in front of him, for several minutes while a crowd of people gathered around. Suddenly he swung his gun up and the people fell back, out of his way. He got up and ran to the cab of the locomotive.

"Get this train moving!" he shouted. The engineer waved and blew the whistle, signaling the final boarding. William stood on the platform, gun in hand and waited. Some people got on the train while others didn't know what to do. He had fire in his eyes and he was going to take his revenge for his brother's death; all he had to do was wait for that marshal to get here.

Silver had jumped back on his horse and rode up to where Rachel lay on the ground. He stepped down and knelt next to her still, lifeless body.

"Why did you have to ride out here?" he asked. Tears were welling up in his eyes, but he blinked them away. The anger was returning and he looked towards the train as the whistle blew. Getting back on his horse, he pulled out his Winchester. Fully loaded, the rifle was better for up close work and he had a couple of men to kill.

Suddenly, he could see him! William was laying on his side, looking in the other direction. Standing up, he walked closer to the man. Jake raised his gun, pulling back the hammer at the same time. William heard the noise and knew he was in trouble. He turned his head and looked at the marshal.

"Drop the gun," Silver said simply.

William was furious; he could not believe how everything had fallen apart.

"You killed my brother and I'm going to kill you!" he hissed. With that he swung his gun up to fire but he had no chance. Silver pulled his trigger and the gun bucked in his hand. The round hit William right in the heart and he fell back down to the ground.

"It's not fair..." he mumbled as he took his last breath.

Jake walked back over to retrieve his rifle, reloading his Colt as he went. Jacob was waiting for him on the platform.

"He killed Rachel, didn't he?"

"Yes," Jake said softly, "I'm sorry, I couldn't get her to stop."

Silver still had work to do so he looked at the train off in the distance.

"I suppose Colin is on that train?"

Jacob looked up with tears in his eyes, "Yes, I saw him looking out a window as it pulled away."

Silver studied the horse that Jacob was holding. "Can I use that?" he asked, pointing at the red dun. Jacob nodded and handed him the reins. The dun would run faster than his horse and would be able to catch up to the train before it gained too much speed.

Jumping up into the saddle, Silver took off after the train. The horse was fast and took off at a full gallop, leaving a trail of dust in its wake. The train was chugging along steadily and slowly gaining speed. Luckily, there was a slight uphill grade so the train had not traveled very far.

After a few minutes at a full gallop, the horse caught up with the train. The cattle car at the end of the train had no platform, but there was a ladder on the side of the car. Jake reined the horse in closer and reached for the closest rung. Missing the first grab he quickly tried again. He caught the middle rung of the ladder with his hand and then jumped across catching the bottom rung with his foot. The horse, suddenly free of its occupant, moved away from the train and then stopped, looking at the fleeing train with little interest; the field of long prairie grass it found itself in was much more appetizing.

Once he caught his breath, Silver climbed up to the roof of the cattle car. Standing there on top, he kept his legs wide, swaying with the motion of the train. As he looked ahead of him, there were eight more cattle cars before reaching the passenger cars. One was a luxury coach for the V.I.P's that had been in town and the other was a second class passenger car. Ahead of that, there was the baggage and mail car, and then the tender and locomotive.

Silver started walking forward. He soon got the feel of the motion of the train and then started running. Reaching the end of the car, he jumped from one car to the next and ran forward again. As he got closer to the passenger coaches, he tried to come up with a plan. He didn't know where Colin was, so there wasn't much he could do except maybe sneak in and hope to catch him unaware.

When he reached the first passenger car, Jake lay down on the roof and peered underneath, trying to see through the door. He could see plush red fabric on the seats and thick carpeted floors. "This must be the luxury coach," he thought. He swung down onto the rear platform of the car and drew his revolver.

Slowly opening the door he stepped inside. Upon hearing the noise from outside, several people looked back to see who had entered. Silver stood there in the middle of the aisle quickly scanning the folks inside. The passengers started pointing and one woman fainted when she saw the tall man holding a gun.

The marshal started walking forward, looking left and right at the faces as he passed. "Not here," he said to himself. He opened the door at the front of the car and stepped across the platform to the second class coach. He had been unable to sneak in unnoticed before so this time he changed his tactic.

Jake threw open the door and rushed inside. He shouted, "Colin Machen!" and looked around for a reaction. Two women screamed when they saw him and several of the men put their hands up, thinking it was a holdup. Only one man didn't turn around. Colin sat still, his hand reaching for the Webley revolver he kept under his jacket.

Suddenly, he turned and fired two quick shots that went wild. Everyone on the train ducked for cover behind the seats. Jake also dove for cover as soon as he saw Colin make his move. Looking back up just in time to see him running for the door, Silver let off a shot at the fleeing man, splintering the wood as the bullet hit the door frame.

Quickly running forward, Silver threw open the door, ready for anything. He peeked outside and saw nothing. Reaching around the side of the car, he grabbed hold of the ladder and started climbing up. He looked across the roof of the railroad car and saw Colin at the same time Colin saw him. The bandit had been making his way down the roof to the other end of the car. When he saw the marshal, he turned and fired again. The bullet struck the roof and ricocheted off with a whizzing sound. Jake ducked back and waited. Colin jumped across to the next car and kept running down the train. Jake jumped up onto the roof of the car and shot again at the fleeing man. His shots missed; it was difficult to aim with the swaying of the train. Colin turned and returned fire as well, his shots missing their mark. He then leapt across to the cattle cars and kept running to the end of the train.

"Where does he think he's going to go?" Jake asked himself.

Taking his time, Silver walked along the roof of the train cars, reloading his gun as he went. When he was ready, he knelt down and took careful aim. Waiting for the swaying of the train to line up with his target, he fired. The bullet struck low, hitting Colin in the leg; the man went down just as he had reached the end of the last car.

Colin rolled down to the edge of the roof. He would have fallen off except the ladder was there. He reached around and lowered himself down slowly, using just one leg. When he got to the bottom, he looked at the ground for a moment. "Better than dyin'," he thought, and let go. He hit the ground hard and rolled to a stop. There were some cuts from rolling through some small rocks but otherwise he was okay. He dusted himself off and gathered his gun, broke it open, and ejected the spent shells. Slowly he slipped one round in after another and replaced the gun in his belt. The wound in his leg was starting to throb with pain so he pulled out his handkerchief, tore it in half, and tied it around the bleeding hole.

As he stood there he wondered which way he should start walking. South Plains was out of the question and Denver was too far. Maybe he should head east, but he was unsure of how far it was to the next town. There were several small towns to the northwest so he figured he would head there. He took a deep breath to steady himself and turned to start walking.

Colin only took one step. Marshal Jake Silver was standing forty feet away, in the middle of the tracks, waiting.

"End of the line, Colin. Show me that gun and pull it out real slow." Colin stood there dumbfounded. "How in the hell did he get here?" he thought, the man didn't even look dirty from jumping off a train!

Colin stood there immobile. He had thoughts racing through his mind, trying to figure a way out of this dilemma.

"There's only one way out," he thought, and he went for his gun. Silver saw him move and in a flash he pulled his revolver. The gun spat out three rounds in a single second. Colin stood there, his gun only half way up; suddenly he couldn't raise it any further. Looking down at his chest he saw three small holes, the blood was starting to seep out, spreading down his shirt. He looked back up, his mouth open in shock. He saw Silver standing there, his gun still pointed at him, a wisp of smoke drifting out of the end of the barrel. It was the last thing he saw; Colin fell forward, dead before he hit the ground.

Chapter Thirteen

Marshal Silver was in the sheriff's office with Sheriff Murphy. The two men had spent the last two hours reviewing the events of the past few days. Silver had to write a report for his boss when he returned and he wanted to make sure everything was in order.

The whole town was abuzz, gossiping and re-telling the story of what had happened yesterday. Rachel Kilbourne had been killed by Daniel, Black had really been Marshal Silver, and there had been a gang of bank robbers living in their town for months! Some were amazed that the Kilbourne brothers had been helping the marshal, seeing as how they were Quakers, but everyone was talking about how the bank was robbed without any money being stolen.

"The banker, Mr. Schmidt, figures that they would have taken around two hundred thousand," Sheriff Murphy said, "They had forged those bank books so well that they looked like the real thing."

Silver looked across the desk at the sheriff, "Yeah, I spoke to him this morning; he said it would take him a week to audit the books and make sure everything is back in order."

Silver gathered his notes and put them in his bag. Standing up he reached across and shook the sheriff's hand. "I appreciate your help with everything. I know you didn't believe me about the gang being in town, but you helped anyway and that says a lot. Plus you took a bullet in the arm---how's that feeling by the way?"

Murphy rubbed his aching arm, "It's not too bad, I'll be up and around in a day. Are you going to stay for the funeral?"

"No," Silver replied, "I've got to catch that train before it leaves."

He really could have taken another day, but he didn't want to face the crowd or have to think about his part in getting Rachel killed. The Kilbournes had told him it wasn't his fault but he still felt guilty. Jake didn't let it show, but he was also mourning the loss. It was amazing the deep feelings that had developed for Rachel in just a few days. He just wanted to get away from this place and put it all behind him.

Before he left the office, he tossed an envelope on the desk. "Will you see that Isaac and Jacob get that? It's the money I owe them for their help." With that he turned and walked out, leaving the sheriff sitting at his desk, wondering if this man really was as cold as he seemed.

U.S. Deputy Marshal Jake Silver left town the same way he came in a week earlier. The storm clouds were gathering, growing darker by the minute as they came off the distant mountains. The rain started to pour and he kicked his horse into a fast walking gait, heading towards the railroad depot. On the other side of town, a bolt of lighting hit, followed shortly by a clap of thunder that rolled through town. As the marshal rode over the rise, he disappeared just as suddenly as he had appeared a week earlier.

Several days later, Paul Schmidt was removing the remaining stacks of cash from the safe to send them to the main bank in Denver. He piled them one by one in the strong box until it was almost full. Just as he was about to grab the last stack of bills, a feather fell out and floated down to the floor. It was a duck feather, such as a gentleman would wear in his hat. Paul picked it up and studied it for a moment, "I wonder how that got in there?" he asked himself. He stuck it in his shirt pocket and closed up the safe. He whistled softly to himself, confident that no one could ever successfully rob his bank.

DATE DUE